no

time

to

die

also by grace f. edwards

In the Shadow of the Peacock

If I Should Die

A Toast Before Dying

doubleday

new york
london
toronto
sydney
auckland

no
time
to
die

grace f. edwards

a mali anderson mystery

PUBLISHED BY DOUBLEDAY
a division of Random House, Inc.
1540 Broadway, New York, New York 10036

DOUBLEDAY and the portrayal of an anchor with a dolphin
are trademarks of Doubleday, a division of
Random House, Inc.

Book design by Donna Sinisgalli.

Library of Congress Cataloging-in-Publication Data

Edwards, Grace F. (Grace Frederica)
No time to die / Grace Edwards. — 1st ed.
p.   cm.
I. Title.
PS3555.D99N68   1999
813'.54—dc21   98-56014
                                               CIP

ISBN 0-385-49247-2
Copyright © 1999 by Grace F. Edwards
All Rights Reserved
Printed in the United States of America
July 1999
First Edition
1   3   5   7   9   10   8   6   4   2

for the members of

the harlem writers guild

and

perri and simone

My thanks to the Harlem Writers Guild, Inc., especially Donis Ford, Bill Banks, Sarah Elizabeth Wright, Betty Ann Jackson, Sheila Doyle, and Alphonso Nicks for their insight, support, and friendship.

no

time

to

die

prologue

At eight o'clock 140th Street was unusually quiet for a
Wednesday evening in June. And empty. The man made his
way past the Mahalia Jackson school cradling the small package in the crook of his arm like a gift. He was of average
height but his arms were well developed, unusually muscular
in contrast to his thin, dark brown frame.

The light from the vacant school yard shone through the
high chain-link fence to cast his fractured image on the pave-

ment. His shadow stretched before him, longer and thinner, then faded altogether as he moved beyond the light.

Take it easy, Ache. Ain't no need to rush. You know how you get. Nearly got caught last time. Easy . . .

He turned onto Edgecombe Avenue and, except for a couple walking a small dog near St. Mark's Church two blocks away, the avenue was also empty. Then he remembered the storm everyone said was coming. This made him smile as he approached the house, a well-kept five-story red brick walkup with a marble entrance.

He made his way up the short flight of steps carefully, then paused in the lobby as if he had come for a visit.

Here's the bell. Check the time. Little past eight. Late, but not too. Intercom working . . .

"Yes, Miss Hastings? I'm from the supermarket. A package was left out of your delivery and I thought I'd bring it over . . . No, ma'am. No trouble at all."

The sound in his left ear seemed louder now, more distinct.

You see, Ache. She told you ain't no trouble at all. Just open the door. Buzz us in . . . Yes.

Carpeted hallway. Bitch livin' large. But this is it. Walk slow. Quiet. Nobody'll hear nuthin' . . .

Not a sound . . . Now, don't rush. Her door's opening before we even knock.

He stared at the woman standing before him, inhaled her faint jasmine scent, then felt the sweat gather again at the small of his back and in the folds of his shrunken scrotum.

Man, what a fine sister. Beautiful. Just the way I—

"Why, that's very thoughtful of you. I didn't even realize the box was missing."

You hear that, Ache? She ain't even know the box was missin'. Like she supposed to know. Shit! Take care of the bitch . . .

"Okay! Okay!"

"What? Are you all right?"

He blinked, trying to bring her back in focus. Trying to remember what he'd come to do. The perfume, it threw him off.

"I mean—yes, ma'am, it happens like that sometimes. We forget things when we rushing. You probably woulda noticed it in the morning though—at breakfast."

"You're right. Thank you."

She's about to close the door . . . What you waitin' for? Move in. Now.

"Could I trouble you for a glass of water, please?"

"Not at all. I remember seeing you at the checkout. Would you like some ice? Today was a real scorcher and that storm still hasn't come. We need some relief soon. So hot so early in the season. This heat is a killer."

Yeah, it sure is. Smile and say yeah. Follow through the living room. Make sure she's alone. But you can feel it. You can usually tell . . . Not like that last place. When that dude answered the hall phone, had to back the fuck outta there fast . . . Yeah, so this is the kitchen . . . Shit, she lookin' kinda solid, bigger than you thought, but not too tall. You can handle her . . . Wait till she turns her back, opens the freezer. Get her hands on the ice tray. That's it. Now!

Piano. Wire. The. Best. Way. Loop it twice so ain't no sound. Shit, she stronger . . . than she looked. Up against the fridge. Knee in her back. That's it. Pull . . . tight.

But she continued to struggle, twist, flail, and the man felt his grip loosening on the wire. The pounding in his throat reached his ears. His arms ached and for a split second he thought about letting go and using his razor, but he quickly reconsidered. Piano wire was the best. *Soldier of Fortune* said so. Always the best. Besides, it had worked all those other times . . .

Then the moment he'd planned, schemed, and dreamed about: he heard the hard snap and saw the spray of saliva streak red across the door of the fridge and the hood of the stove next to it. It painted the yellow canisters of sugar, flour, tea, and coffee and finally she dropped her arms and he felt her knees give way. A second later she sagged heavily against him.

That's it, that's it, that's it. Tongue's out. Purple. Way it supposed to be . . . Now things'll be quiet again. Right, Ache? Things'll be quiet. Go on, Ache. Let's see how she do with her tongue hangin' out. Remember how that last bitch did you? Go on. Show her.

chapter

one

I rested my arms on the window and glanced out at a late afternoon sky that resembled rusted steel. Threatening clouds had been hanging low for three days now and so far the weatherman had not earned his keep.

The Saturday crowd moving along 125th Street probably had as little faith in the forecast as I and went about business as usual, ignoring the heat and the haze.

I sneaked another glance at my watch and wondered how long Elizabeth was going to wait. It was nearly 6:30.

"Claudine should've been here by now," I said, trying but failing to hide my impatience. "As long as we've known her, she's always been late, but this is something special."

I was annoyed because we three had arranged a week ago to go out to dinner to celebrate her impending liberation. I knew James Thomas, her soon-to-be ex, and I had detested him from the day we confronted each other three years ago at their wedding reception.

Now I pictured his smooth face and silky soft voice and felt a fleeting panic, imagining that he might have talked Claudine into changing her mind about the divorce, that he would get a job again, stop drinking, stop blaming and beating her for what he imagined the world was doing to him.

I turned from the window and faced into the office to watch Elizabeth lean back in her chair, an old swivel model of glossy dark walnut and vintage leather upholstery. The chair had belonged to her father when he'd had his own law practice uptown over the old Smalls Paradise next door to the Poro School of Beauty Culture. That was years ago. Elizabeth's office was smaller, and probably a lot more expensive. Space on 125th Street near the Apollo didn't come cheap.

The coil beneath the chair squeaked as she leaned forward. She pushed her cascade of brown dreadlocks away from her face and folded her arms on the desk.

"Calm down, Mali. I don't know if you're annoyed because Claudine's late or because of the advice I just offered you. We can discuss this another time if you'd like. I only want you to understand that if you have to attend another hearing, you may very well lose the case. There's a new police commissioner on the job; the city claims it's trying to save money, and the cop—the principal in your lawsuit—is now dead. The department's offering you reinstatement and a possible promotion for helping break that drug ring."

I listened and allowed her voice to trail into a familiar silence before I answered. As an attorney, Elizabeth Jackson had a very good reputation and a practice lucrative enough to afford a four-story brownstone near Marcus Garvey Park. My dad knew her father and she and I had gone to school together. She went into law and I opted for social work—except I'd taken a short detour into the NYPD and gotten fired for punching out a racist cop.

When I answered, it was the same reply she'd heard since taking the case.

"Possible promotion? Possible? Sounds like a word game to me. That's not the best they can do and they know it. I'm not backing down and I'm not compromising. You know as well as I that I have no intention of rejoining the department."

I watched her shrug. "I can understand that. Why you joined in the first place will always be a mystery to me."

She caught my stare and quickly said, "Okay, I'm just letting you know what the situation is; what you stand to lose."

"I'll take the chance," I said, and turned to look out of the window again.

I'd planned to enter the social work doctoral program at

NYU. To hell with rejoining NYPD. Just show me Mr. Benjamin Franklin and all of his brothers. They'll help with my tuition.

I gazed at the Apollo's marquee, which hung like a dark outcropping over the crowd moving below. The theater was once known as Hurtig and Seaman's Music Hall, a vaudeville house catering to white audiences. It reopened in 1934 as a showcase for black entertainment, and the new owners renamed it the Apollo. Benny Carter's band played the opening, Ralph Cooper was the M.C., and there were sixteen dancers called the Hot Steppers.

My father, a self-named Harlem historian as well as a jazz musician, tells me this stuff. He remembers a lot and spends his free time entertaining me with information he says I should have if I'm to be an authentic Harlemite. I thought I was authentic enough, having been born thirty-two years ago in Harlem Hospital and raised on Strivers' Row.

In addition to the big bands that played the Apollo, Dad also loved the comedy of Moms Mabley, Pigmeat ("Here Comes the Judge") Markham, and early Redd Foxx, who later sanitized his act for TV. Ella Fitzgerald got her start here, winning the Amateur Hour with "A-Tisket, A-Tasket," a song someone advised her not to sing because "it didn't have enough rhythm for black folks."

I turned away from the marquee and stared down the street, looking for Claudine in the crowd. The thoroughfare was clogged with the end-of-day confusion of buses and cars. I did not spot her familiar face and I glanced at my watch again. Nearly seven o'clock. Two hours overdue. Elizabeth had left three messages on Claudine's machine.

"When did you last speak to her?" I asked.

"Few days ago. To confirm dinner."

"I think we should head on up to her place," I sighed. "See what's going on."

The temperature had dropped a few degrees but the humidity still hung like a blanket as we strolled up Frederick Douglass Boulevard. Before we approached the Sugar Shack near 139th Street, my silk dress was clinging in all the wrong places and I regretted having worn it. Cotton would have deflected some of the more pointed observations of the stoop loungers. We passed the restaurant and waved to the manager, who was chatting with a crowd of Asian tourists.

"We'll be a bit late," I said to him, smiling.

"Don't worry about it. We'll hold your reservation. Seven o'clock, right?"

At 140th Street young girls were jumping rope in the Mahalia Jackson school yard, ignoring the heat radiating up through their Keds. Two teams—one jumping double Dutch and the other jumping straight rope—tried to outperform each other with in-the-air splits, double skips, and what looked like pretzel twists before feet touched the ground again. They performed like Olympic aspirants and I wondered why they had no audience.

We turned the corner onto Edgecombe Avenue and the crowd around Claudine's building surprised me.

No one, for the short time she'd lived here, had ever sat, leaned, lounged, or otherwise "hung" on her stoop. The kids played in the school yard and the grown-ups lounged on the benches in St. Nicholas Park a block away.

Perhaps it was the polished brass trim around the doors, the ornate knobs, or the trace of the arc in the stonework above the entrance that suggested an elegant canopy had once stretched to the curb. Now the entrance was so crowded we had to work our way through.

Several people looked at us expectantly and I felt a pull in the pit of my stomach. In the lobby the odor hit like a fist in the face. It was the smell of something or someone rotting and I began to sweat even as I rushed up the stairs. I wanted to shut down all my senses against that peculiar odor that let me know there was a body near.

On the fourth floor Mr. William, the super, held out his arms. "Miss Mali, I guess you don't want to go any further."

"What happened?"

He shook his head and I stared at him, my throat suddenly gone dry. "Mr. William, what happened?"

"I don't know, but somethin' ain't right in your friend's apartment. I ain't seen her in a couple a days now—usually see her go joggin' when I'm out sweepin', you know—but for a couple days now, people been complainin' about the smell.

I ain't got a key so I called the cops. Oughtta be here any minute."

I looked at Elizabeth leaning against the wall. Her eyes were closed and beads of sweat covered her forehead. Mr. William saw her also. "Whyn't y'all go on back downstairs and wait." His voice was soft and consoling, as if he already knew what I refused to even imagine.

"Ain't nuthin' else to do . . ." he said gently.

I held onto Elizabeth's arm, not so much to guide her as to steady myself, and retreated down the stairs and into the street.

"Maybe it's from another apartment," Elizabeth whispered as we moved back through the crowd. I didn't answer because I knew better. Of the four apartments on the floor, only Claudine's had the mat of flies covering the door.

People stared as we passed and there was a silence about them that I tried to ignore. We moved away from the building to the curb, where I finally drew a breath so deep my chest hurt.

The ambulance and the squad car turned the corner at the same time with sirens blaring. The rotating lights splashed over us as the officers and EMS technicians disappeared inside.

Minutes later Elizabeth tapped my arm. "Mali . . ." Her voice was soft as she pointed, and I turned to watch another car pull up behind the squad car. Detective Tad Honeywell stepped out. He spotted me before I called.

"What's going on, Mali? You all right?"

"I . . . don't know. I won't know until I find out what's causing the odor. Super thinks it's apartment 4G, where my friend Claudine lives."

"You were up there?"

"Yes. We three were supposed to have dinner together."

"When did you last speak to her?"

"Three days ago," Elizabeth said. "And I left a message yesterday and two messages earlier today."

Tad shook his head but he had already taken on that professional cover and I could read nothing in his expression.

"I'll be back in a few minutes."

He made his way through the crowd, which had grown larger, drawn by the spinning lights of the squad car and ambulance. I moved to the other side of the avenue, taking Elizabeth with me. The intersection of 140th Street and Edgecombe was now blocked and traffic had to detour. Several minutes later the EMS workers came back through the crowd, placed their kits in the ambulance, and pulled away.

Tad emerged from the building and walked toward us, moving slowly, shaking his head. The odor had saturated his clothing and I wondered how close he was able to get before he had to turn away.

"Is it 4G?" I asked, not wanting to say Claudine's name.

"Yeah. I'm sorry, Mali. I'm sorry."

Elizabeth put her hands to her head and I held her shoulders and began to cry. The three of us had been friends. Claudine had first been a friend of my older sister, Benin, whom she'd met in graduate school. My sister died in Europe several years ago. Claudine had taught school in Philadelphia for a while, then returned to New York. The times we'd gone out, she'd talked so much about Benin that I'd come home close to tears. I looked at Tad now and asked, "What . . . happened to her?"

"Strangulation."

"What?"

"Wire."

I stood there in the fading light of the early evening, not wanting to understand what I'd just heard.

"A wire?"

I turned to Elizabeth but her wide eyes only confirmed what I didn't want to believe. Through the fog of shock, Tad's voice came to me: "I'm putting you two in a cab. I'll call you as soon as I can, Mali. I'm sorry."

"No!" I backed away. "No cab! No nothing!" I screamed, watching the surprise and confusion as Elizabeth moved toward me. "No!"

I turned and ran toward the building, tearing through the crowd and muscling my way around the patrolman near the stairs. I heard a voice, Tad saying, "Let her go! She can see it."

I ran up four flights, with my hand against my mouth, which did not help at all. The odor was at once powerful, numbing. If it was Claudine, I wanted to see her, connect her to it; otherwise I'd wonder the rest of my life how it happened. As I'd been left to wonder about Benin. Tad was behind me but did not try to restrain me.

I made my way to the kitchen, almost dizzy from lack of

air, then leaned against the table and stared. A chair had been overturned, the canisters on the counter near the fridge were covered with dried black stains. The body on the floor was Claudine but I only recognized the bathrobe I had given her as a birthday present last year, pale pink silk with a corded belt with tassles on the end.

The robe had been spread open, her stomach a mountain of gas, and her face flattened as if a steamroller had gone over it. Her features had disintegrated in the humidity. On her face where her mouth once was were flakes of some kind. Cereal. It had been scattered in her eyes, ears, nose, and mouth. It was on her chest and between her sprawled legs.

I fell back against Tad and a minute later found myself back out in the street, sitting on the curb, staring, Elizabeth shouting, and Tad pressing a handkerchief against my mouth as I retched until my stomach was on fire.

chapter

two

"Turn that fuckin' radio off! How long we got to listen to the news? You hoppin' and jumpin' from 'INS to CBS every time they mention that girl gettin' strangled. Got it blastin' so loud, who the hell was she, anyway? Your dumb-ass girl-friend?"

Hazel's laughter stopped long enough for her to raise the forty-ounce bottle of Colt 45 to her swollen face. She stood in the doorway of her son's room and he could hear the loud swallowing from where he lay on his bed, hoping, praying, that maybe this time she'd misswallow and the liquid would rush down the wrong pipe. He glared at her upturned arm, and in the dim light, imagined a ham with the fat clinging to it, sliding along the meat rack at a slaughterhouse.

"And another thing, when you gonna git to this room? Smell like a shithouse in here. Now you got you a little jay-oh-bee again, it done gone to your head and you takin' showers two times a day, but don't tell me you can't smell this dirt."

He sat up on the edge of his bed, stiff as a soldier at reveille, still gazing at his mother. Her 350-pound bulk crowded the door, blocking out what light there was. And he could feel rage and terror competing for space within him.

Shithouse. Like she one to talk. I know she here before I even put my key in the door. When the fuck was the last time she seen water? Maybe two, no, three months ago? And that punk-ass boyfriend had to call the fire department to jack her out the tub. From then on, it was "bird baths'" as she like to call it.

He wanted to squeal with laughter, but fright held the sound to the back of his throat. Bird baths. There was no bird on earth, in fact or fiction, that resembled this woman. Except maybe something roaming Jurassic Park. And then you'd need a double-size wraparound drive-in movie screen to get the full picture. No wonder the fuckin' dumb boyfriend split. Probably figured what little he was snatchin' from her check wasn't worth it.

He bit his tongue and kept his shaking hands balled at his sides as he watched her drain the bottle and luxuriate in a long-drawn-out belch. Her stubby fingers pushed the Dutch-bob wig from her sweating face and then jabbed at him.

"Now, you throw your ass down from your shoulder and git this room in some kinda shape. 'Cause you got a piece a job again don't cut no ice. Ain't no maid service in here!"

He remained silent, thinking: *It ain't about no maid service. It ain't about that and she know it. Not the way her room lookin'. Even the roaches 'fraid to step in there . . .*

She turned away and he watched her waddle back down the hall. He could hear her moving through the living room past the battered sofa resting on the six cinder blocks; the two milk crates with the thin piece of Formica tattooed with cigarette burns that served as a coffee table. The tattoos were no longer visible beneath the pile of Chinese takeout cartons and moldy pizza boxes.

He heard her curse and kick empty beer cans out of her path. The television, broken for the last three days and resting on a pyramid of plastic crates, would probably be the next target. She had cursed at it too many days. It was time to do more.

He heard the crash and didn't move, but waited to find out if she had fallen. Even if she had, he didn't intend to do anything. Except to step over her on his way out of the dark smelly place. But the other, private voice was quiet. Nobody told him he had to go out.

So he crept forward only far enough to close his bedroom door and muffle the sound of the cursing. Then he sprawled back against the greasy pillows. *Naw. Ain't goin' nowhere. Not tonight. I'm on the news. How 'bout that. Just like last time. I'm on the news . . . Keep this up, I be on Geraldo!*

chapter

three

I stood with Elizabeth near the curb outside of Benta's Funeral Home less than two blocks from where Claudine had lived and watched a bank of clouds scatter before the light wind. The sun broke through in white, midday brilliance, and I knew if Claudine were alive, we'd be planning a quick run out to Jones Beach. Instead, we were about to head uptown to Woodlawn Cemetery. Woodlawn. With a sealed bronze box covered with bouquets of roses, wreaths, sprays of lilacs.

Last year around this time Elizabeth and I had gone to a

weekend party at Sag Harbor where Claudine had finally agreed to wear a thigh-high two-piece swimsuit while Elizabeth and I sported the thong thing. Claudine was five-six with braided hair so thick that folks thought she'd had someone else's hair woven in. She had walked along the beach that day in her deep orange two-piece with her hands on her hips and her head bent against the breeze, smiling.

The water eddied around her ankles, and her brown skin had sparkled where the spray hit. Two guys, mid-thirties but just entering adolescence, it seemed, trailed behind her, emerging from their trance long enough to playfully elbow each other out of the way.

They must have called out or said something because she'd turned to face them and her laughter drifted back to where Elizabeth and I sat on the blanket. We looked at each other, then at Claudine again. She was laughing, soft and spontaneous, not so much at the antics but finally laughing her way out of the box that her husband had beaten her into.

She had shone, had actually begun to move away from what she'd gone through with James. The two guys came back with her to the blanket, and when Claudine pulled a bottle of Veuve Clicquot from the cooler and couldn't find extra glasses, Brandon, the one who'd introduced himself first, must have set a record racing to the beach house to get some. Claudine had watched him and laughed again, laughed until her eyes filled.

"You think it was James, don't you?" Elizabeth said, interrupting my reverie. "I can see it in your face that you think it was him. You know how wild he'd gotten when she had him served with the papers."

She'd suggested this several times over the last few days, even as we went through the motions of helping Claudine's parents with the funeral arrangements. I even contacted Brandon, who had opened the champagne that day and who had been e-mailing her every day since then. He'd been shocked into silence, and when he caught his breath, he said, "Not Claudine. Not her. What happened?"

I had no answer.

The *Daily Challenge* and the *Amsterdam News* had come up with their own theories, but it was speculation. There were no clues—at least none that the papers knew about.

The service ended and I watched Claudine's parents emerge from the dim interior of the funeral home. Mrs. Hastings held her husband's arm, her face a map of anguish as she walked toward the limousine. Yesterday at home, she couldn't contain her bewilderment when she finally held the obituary and began to read it as if it had belonged to someone else. Then she pronounced Claudine's name and birth date, and the scream that came did not stop until the doctor arrived.

Later, when she had dropped into a fitful sleep, Mr. Hastings left her bedside and approached me. He was tall, reed-thin, and usually stood straight as a rod. Now he was shaking, as if sixty-seven years of life had sneaked up from behind and knocked him sideways. Even his voice wavered. "Mali, you were once a cop. What . . . ? How . . . ?"

He raised his hands, trying to pull the answer from the air, then lowered them to hold onto my arm. I felt the tremor through my jacket sleeve. "Listen, Mali." He softened his voice and nodded toward the bedroom where his wife lay oblivious of the activity going on around her. "My old queen will grieve herself into her grave, right behind our child. God knows I can't let that happen. Somebody's got to do something . . ."

The only times I'd seen an older man cry was when Dad broke down at Mom's funeral and again at the news of my sister Benin's death. Mom had been so healthy, a nonsmoker, a dancer, walker, jogger, but in an instant her heart had pumped that erratic, extra beat and taken her away.

Benin and her husband died in a hiking accident in Europe. I thought of them now as I watched Mr. Hastings and knew it was too late, too useless, to ask how death could arrive so quickly and in so many guises.

Elizabeth and I watched the rest of the mourners step forward to enlarge the crowd gathered in tight nervous knots. Deborah, our longtime friend, who had flown in from Washington, stepped from the door and moved toward us. Her face was swollen, as if the tears hadn't stopped from the moment I'd called with the news.

No greetings, only whispered amazement that something like this could have happened. Claudine's building was supposed to be safe. The lobby door was always locked. Just as her own door was supposed to have been.

"Mali. Elizabeth. How could this . . . how could something like this happen? Claudine was . . ."

I held her arm and moved toward Elizabeth's car a few feet away. Once seated inside, Deborah leaned back and closed her eyes. I saw fear imprinted on her face and a faint trace of the scar on her neck—the result of a push-in robbery that caused her to abandon the city for Washington. She had planned to return, but now with this latest circumstance, I doubted it. I watched the tremor in her hands and wondered if it had been a good idea to have called her at all. But we were old friends. She would have wanted to know.

Elizabeth tapped my arm and I stepped away from the car. "You do think it was James. I can see it in your face."

I didn't answer but concentrated on the traffic, which had slowed to a crawl. I scanned the cars, then glanced across the avenue and spotted Tad sitting in his car near St. James Church. He inclined his head slightly when our eyes met, and a minute later he pulled away, heading downtown.

My breath caught in my throat as I remembered how he'd pulled me away from the bloated form in the kitchen. He had put his hand over my mouth and nose and kept me from throwing up.

I turned back to Elizabeth. "I don't know what to think. James was capable of some really bad stuff. I mean the things that girl went through, I can't believe she stayed in the marriage as long as she did. The first black eye should've been the last."

I spoke quietly so that Deborah wouldn't hear but I grew angrier thinking of James Thomas, who was still inside. He had shown up late, eased his way into a front-row seat, and when one of Mrs. Hastings's friends rose to sing Claudine's favorite song, James had fallen to his knees in a flood of grief loud enough to drown out the solo. If the casket had been open, he surely would've tried to climb in.

Glances were exchanged among those who knew about the abuse, and I heard a few patient sighs. I had been so angry I brushed past Dad, ignoring his frown, and walked out. Elizabeth had joined me outside a few minutes later. I concentrated on the crowd again in an effort to shake away the thought of James's performance.

I recognized some of Claudine's colleagues from the high school where she'd taught, and thought of the impact on her students in September, and wondered if grief counselors would be available the same way they were provided in the more affluent districts. Her neighbors and other familiar faces from Edgecombe Avenue filed out, and the doors of limos and private cars swung open.

James now stepped out of the building, trailing the pack, blinking rapidly as if unaccustomed to functioning in daylight. The dark suit hung loose on his five-foot, eight-inch frame, and sunlight caught the telltale wrinkles and worn cuffs. This convinced me he had scrounged it at the last minute, probably from one of his drinking buddies.

He twisted his sweat-stained straw hat in his hands, inspecting the crowd, prepared to further stretch his performance on anyone willing to watch. He glanced at me and I stared until his gaze faltered and fell away.

The cars were filling up. Dad had gotten in another car. Elizabeth was driving and I climbed in beside her. Bertha Owen, my friend and favorite hairdresser, approached, rapped on the window, then climbed in to sit beside Deborah. "Girl, how you doin'? I didn't know you were in town."

"I came for the service. Mali called. I . . . I . . . ."

Bertha reached over and gathered her in her arms. "Poor baby. Nobody knows why these things happen but they do. Claudine's restin' now. Restin'."

I turned to add my own words of comfort and found Bertha glaring at me, as if asking how I could have told Deborah, knowing what she had experienced. I swallowed my words and turned away.

Other car doors opened and slammed. Through the window I watched James twist the hat as he shifted from one foot to the other. His once slickly handsome face now seemed ragged with humiliation as the cortege glided from the curb in a veil of silence. Elizabeth's car was last in line and I turned to look. James stared back and held the battered hat at an angle. His frown melted into a hollow grin as he shook his fist.

I closed my eyes and murmured something and Elizabeth tapped my arm.

"Are you all right?"

"Yes. Yes." I stared ahead, not trusting myself to say any more. The car in front lost focus and I blinked hard, trying to fight the feeling boiling in my chest.

James had killed Claudine. I was sure of it. He was a psychopath because how else to reconcile the scene in Claudine's apartment with the image of him howling on his knees in front of the casket.

I still could not bring myself to tell Elizabeth what I'd seen. Or how I really felt about James. Perhaps later, after the pain and heartache of the wake, after Deborah had returned to Washington to deal with new fears and nightmares, I could probably talk. But not now. The wound was too deep.

chapter

four

"You don't want to talk about it," Tad whispered, "but I have
to go over this 'cause maybe there's something you might
remember. Maybe someone was in the crowd around Claudine's that night who might've caught your eye. Or maybe
there's something about James you might've forgotten."

His voice was soft but insistent and I turned from the
balcony, wishing I could forget everything about James. The
sun, already setting, left a fast-fading gold wash against the
gray stone walls of the Riverbend complex. Tad's fourteenth-

floor apartment faced out over the calm of the Harlem River and the bustle of the Drive below. Across the river, the tracks of Metro-North stretched past. To the north of the complex, the steel webbing of the 145th Street and 155th Street Bridges gleamed in the dying light, and the Willis Avenue Bridge to the south cast a latticed shadow on the water.

Tad leaned against the terrace door, and behind him, the living room was already in shadow. I could not distingush the chairs or even the sofa I'd been sitting on just ten minutes ago. He stepped onto the terrace and I regarded his deep brown skin and even deeper eyes, and—the rare occasions when he smiled—teeth so perfect they didn't seem real.

I wondered why we tended to praise perfection by comparing it to something unreal.

His teeth, his smile, his strong arms, everything about him was authentic and substantial, and for a small moment, this vision pulled me away from the gnawing cavity within me. But only for a moment. Tad was patient and quiet but still in that persistent, tenacious, encircling mode.

"Claudine was my sister's friend," I said, "and after Benin died, she sort of hooked onto me when she returned from Philadelphia. She asked me to be her maid of honor and . . ."

I said nothing more and he looked at me.

"And were you?"

"Yes," I said, suddenly tired by the questions. "All I know is that they were married for three years but she only lived with him for a year. He'd hit her on three different occasions that I know of. She left him and he started phoning, begging, and finally threatening her if she didn't come back to him. Even after he'd started seeing someone else, he still phoned, calling her his wife even after she'd dropped her married name and referred to herself as Hastings."

"There's no record of an order of protection under either name," Tad said. "Did she ever mention it—that she was going to get one? Or thought about getting one?"

I shrugged and turned again to look out over the water. The river traffic was quiet for a Saturday evening. No sails, tugs, and only one Circle Line, but there were plenty of birds. Gulls mostly, with gray-white wings spread wide, passively drifting on a downwind. To the north, the cars had come to a standstill on the 155th Street Bridge.

What did it matter if Claudine had had an order of protection? What was it—a piece of paper. To do what? Flash it in front of her husband's fist like a silver cross before a vampire?

I had felt foolish even suggesting it to her.

"No," she'd said quietly. "No. I'm out of his reach. Out of his orbit now. He'll yell and scream for a time but after a while, he'll quit. Go on to something else. When he calls, I hear his voice, I hang up without a word. He's running out of steam. He only called once this week."

That had been two weeks before she was killed. A piece of paper wouldn't have meant a thing.

"You see," Tad said, "I'm trying to figure out if James was motivated to do something as violent as that. We brought him in three times for questioning and we never mentioned what we found on the body. And unless he's a genuine psychopath, he seemed to have no idea how she really died; kept telling us to check out her new man—the one she'd left him for. But he couldn't even describe him. No name, address, nothing."

"There was no new man," I said, "because Claudine didn't have time to recuperate from the old one. She was too busy changing locks, getting her life back on track, and getting a new wardrobe—he'd cut up her clothes after accusing her of sneaking out on him. The man is crazy and he's a coward. He only seems to want to fight women."

"I know. You said he'd hit his girlfriend."

"A few years ago. It's on file. I answered the call. Domestic disturbance. By the time we arrived, he'd gotten in the wind. Talks loud and runs fast. I wish I could've caught up with him that night."

Tad glanced at me and placed his hands over my balled fists. "Okay, what do you say we take time out?"

He leaned on the balcony with his arm around me and we remained quiet for several minutes, thinking different thoughts. The traffic making its way to the stadium still crawled on the bridge. The Yankees were playing a home game and the grid of lights rippled across the water like a beacon.

Tad cleared his throat and nudged me. "You know, I still make the finest martinis uptown. How about it? Or would you prefer Absolut and orange?"

"Absolut," I said, resting my head on his shoulder.

We remained there until the last remnant of daylight disappeared. The river lost all dimension and the traffic on the Drive dissolved into narrow streams of light merging and dividing at the 135th Street exit.

I wondered how long he was going to let me use his shoulder to cry on. It had been two weeks since the funeral and I still had not adjusted, had not been able to put the phone down fast enough when I realized that, out of habit, I'd dialed Claudine's number. I had to get myself together.

It was warmer in the living room. Several pine-scented candles on the coffee table cast a fragile glow of orange and yellow against the walls.

"Here," he said, "lie down. Stretch out. Let's see if a massage'll help loosen some of the knots. Especially in your shoulders."

The drinks were on the table and he was on his knees unfastening my sandals.

"But I'm gonna start from the bottom," he murmured, "and work my way up."

"Are you . . . stopping along the way?"

"Depends."

"On what?" I asked, already leaning forward to allow him to untie my halter top. His fingers were warm against my skin.

"If I find something around one of these curves, I might brake," he whispered. I felt his mouth move soft against my ankles, my calves, and the underside of my knees.

"Oh. Oh . . . Yes. All right . . ."

He looked at me and I caught his smile, rare and perfect in the radiance of the red and yellow. I removed his shirt and marveled at the way his skin glowed. My fingers trailed an arc around his shoulders and I pulled him to me to taste his mouth. Then I held onto him so tightly I lost my breath, and for the rest of the evening, the first time in a long while, I allowed my eyes to close without crying.

chapter

five

Ache woke up and stared blankly at the lights flashing through his curtainless window. They rotated around the walls like large stars gone awry, painting the ceiling red, white, and red again. He eased out of the narrow bed feeling the prickle of fear, sudden and sharp, slide down his spine.

Cops. There were no sirens but he knew it was the police. He ducked his head below the flashing lights as if they were incoming missiles and crept to the window. Four squad cars had pulled up to the house across the street, a five-story tenement that had been abandoned to the dealers and squatters and others who'd had nowhere else to run.

One car, surrounded by police, was on the sidewalk with headlights beaming into the garbage-strewn hallway. Three more cars were angled at the curb. A crowd, large for 3:00 A.M., had already gathered. Ache folded his muscular arms and leaned on his windowsill, waiting to see who and how many would be brought out this time and if his dealer had been caught in the sweep.

Five minutes later four cops in flak jackets brought two men out. There were no TV cameras, so neither performed the usual perp walk, but one grinned and flicked his tongue for the benefit of the crowd, who howled their support.

"Hold on, brutha. It ain't nuthin' but a ride down and a walk back! Hold on!"

The cops ignored everyone and hustled the two into the car on the sidewalk.

They got Bad Boy again but he oughtta be back before my stash run out. Yeah, two, three days.

He left the window and pulled the sour-smelling mattress back to check the cache: a small bag of weed and the smaller plastic bag of pills and capsules—steroids necessary for his muscle development program.

This'll hold me.

He lay down again and wondered if he should roll a joint to take his mind off the stars painting the walls. He was glad he had woken up because he was getting tired of the dream that seemed to be coming more often lately.

In the dark, wide awake now, it came to him again. Someone was whispering, telling him how slick he was not to have gotten caught yet. And how way back, way back, he'd gotten that name Ache.

He'd been sitting at the dinner table, eight years old and squirming in pants he'd outgrown when he was six, wearing no underwear to speak of, and itching in an old woolen sweater that hadn't seen water in a year.

Hazel, his mother, had slammed her fork down hard, rattling the salt and pepper shakers, and glared at him. "Every time I look at your ugly ass, you make my head ache. You give me a stomachache. Don't need you sittin' here givin' me eye for eye. Make me throw up. Git outta here. You can eat in your room!"

He had melted out of sight, knowing that she would lock him in the closet like the other times if he didn't move fast enough. Occasionally one of her men would turn the key and let him out. But sometimes even they forgot.

One time, when he finally heard the key turn and the door opened again, the moon was already pushing a small dim light through the open window. He had gone to his room, waited until his mother was occupied in her own bed, then crept down the fire escape on his belly, carrying a coil of rope.

No one was around to question an eight-year-old prowling the streets after midnight. No one was there to track him through the backyards and alleys, and by dawn, he had killed seven cats and two stray puppies, left them on clotheslines stretched between sheets and socks.

In another part of the dream, he was in a classroom again, sitting alone in the last row, silent in a class of thirty. He did not hear the teacher call his name because he'd been staring at Mercy Anne Tompkins sitting in front of him. Twelve years old and beautiful. Each day he studied her shining braids, full blouses, short skirts, and patent-leather shoes. When she moved, the scent of the fresh soap he rarely had drifted under his nose. Her large eyes were wide and beautiful even though she never looked at him.

But she turned that day and laughed with everyone else when the teacher cut into him with his usual arsenal of wit: "You raised your hand this morning when I took attendance. Are you really here?"

Mercy Anne with the beautiful eyes had laughed with everyone else.

After school, he couldn't follow her home because a car always came to pick her up. He watched it disappear in the traffic, then turned and walked fast to catch up with Natalie, a small ten-year-old, always smiling, even when no one was around to see her smile. So he caught up with her and she smiled vacantly and sang words in a baby's voice that she herself didn't understand and hid her broken teeth behind her small hands.

He looked at her hair, knotted and gray with lint, her dress too small and too wrinkled, her shoe heels worn to the ground so that the toes curled up. She had no socks to cover ashy legs but she smiled and hummed as he took her hand and led her into a building a block from the school. She followed him to the roof landing, and when she stopped smiling and said she didn't want to play anymore, he'd left her with her neck bent sideways under a discarded box spring mattress, with old paint cans, a wheelless baby stroller, and garbage-filled plastic bags piled on top.

For weeks, he lounged on the stoop watching Natalie's mother wander around, looking in garbage cans, alleys, back-yards, crazed, crying, asking if anyone had seen her little girl.

See what I mean, Ache? You ain't never been caught. You slick.

He lay on the bed watching the flash of the lights and thinking of Mercy Anne until the patrol cars pulled away, plunging the room into darkness again. He smiled and turned over, found a comfortable spot on the sagging mattress, and fell asleep.

chapter

six

James's ex-girlfriend came on the line sounding sleepy, then
more animated when she discovered the caller wasn't someone she didn't want to be bothered with.

"What'd you say your name was?"

"Anderson. Mali Anderson."

"Where do I know you from?"

"I met you a few years ago, Miss Taylor, when I worked at
the precinct and—"

"Precinct? Listen, lady. I don't know no-fuckin'-body at no precinct, understand? And I don't—"

"You remember me, Marie. It was a few years ago, one night in July. Temperature broke over a hundred that day. You were living with James Thomas and we came up to your place on a nine-eleven."

"Yeah, so?"

"I was the officer with the gray eyes. James had skipped by the time we got there and I talked to you about getting an order of protection. We spoke a long time, and when things had quieted, you asked if I was wearing contacts, remember?"

"Oh. Oh, yeah. I sure do. Tall, dark skin, with them pale gray eyes. Ain't that a combination. I sure do remember. I even asked what you doin' hangin' with some lightweight Five-Os when you coulda been a model or somethin'. You still with 'em? Don't tell me you followin' up a complaint two years after the fact. I coulda been dead and risen twice."

"No. That's not why I'm calling. This is something different. The schoolteacher who was murdered two weeks ago."

There was a pause before she said, "Yeah . . . As a matter a fact, I had a visit from a cop, a detective Honey-something."

"Honeywell."

"That's the name. Jesus, was he some fine brother. Asking me a lot a questions about James and all. He was so damn handsome I couldn't even concentrate. I just kept starin'."

There was another pause and I wondered if she was trying

to decide whether to speak to me. When Tad had visited her, she had probably been reluctant—not to protect her ex, but because she, like most folks I know, deeply distrusted anyone in blue with a badge, handsome or not.

"I'm no longer on the force," I said in the silence. "As a matter of fact, I have a lawsuit pending against NYPD."

"You do? Well you go, girl. You all right then. NYPD get away with a lotta shit. I see that badge as just a fuckin' license to fuck over you."

"Well, I no longer have one and I was hoping to speak with you. Meet you somewhere to talk about Claudine."

"You knew James's wife?"

"She was my sister's friend."

"Oh. I'm sorry to hear that. 'Cause what happened to her just wasn't correct, you know what I'm sayin'. It wasn't right. I can't understand why the good always go young and the ones that shoulda croaked is layin' in the cut like they got a long-term lease."

"I know, Marie. It's scary the way she died."

"And you think James done it?"

"I don't know. He wasn't too nice to her while they were together. And her parents are devastated. They're too old to put their lives back together, but if they don't get some answers soon, this will surely take them out of here."

There was another silence, shorter this time, before she spoke again. Her voice was softer. "Well . . . listen. I'll meet you, okay? In the Lido. I usually hang in the Lenox Lounge but sometimes James pop in there and I'm not in the mood to deal with him. And anyway I promised the barmaid at the Lido I'd stop by. Tomorrow is her birthday—Fourth of July— but she celebratin' it tonight so I'm poppin' in around six.''

"Fine. I'll see you.''

The Lido Bar on 125th Street between Malcolm X Boulevard and Fifth Avenue is an old spot that has outlasted the Silver Rail, the Baby Grand, the Celebrity Club, the Midway, Frank's Restaurant, Palm Cafe, Purple Manor, Vincent's Place, and a number of other watering holes along the main artery.

When I stepped in, the barstools on the left were occupied by regulars who didn't swivel an inch when the door opened. The television was perched strategically over the door and a newcomer could be appraised with a flick of a lid up, down, and back to the screen again. No motion to disturb the cool and chill and other casually maintained postures.

Opposite the bar, behind a waist-high wrought-iron railing, a line of tables stretched to the rear. Four men in their sixties, probably retired, were holding court. They smiled and tipped hats as I strolled by to sit at the end of the bar near a small bandstand.

The television sound was off and the regulars watched and nodded soundlessly at a soundless ball game. I ordered an

Absolut and orange with plenty of ice and settled back to catch the talk of the day floating above a vintage Joe Williams 'riff on a jukebox that was probably installed the day the bar opened a long time ago.

Opinions ranged from what type of industrial-strength suntan lotion Michael Jackson would need if he eventually decided to rejoin the tribe, to what O.J. needed to do to redeem himself in the eyes of black folks now that he was no longer living high on the hog in white heaven, but mostly they ragged Michael.

"I'm askin' you," a fat man in the group of four said, "did the Man in the Mirror ever look in the mirror? I don't think so. Ghost scare the livin' shit out you, high noon on Times Square."

"Now, wait a minute," the second man argued, "that boy got more talent in his little toe than you got in your whole watermelon head."

"Well, least my watermelon head is black."

". . . and nappy," chimed someone leaning at the bar.

"Hell, I'm happy I'm nappy but let us get back to the feet. What color is Michael Jackson's little toe?"

"How the hell should I know? And who the hell care what his damn toe look like? With all that surgery, he probably don't have no mo' toe."

"Well, I still say when you got that kinda talent, it entitle you to do stuff other folks can't . . ."

"Includin' makin' a fool a yourself?"

The door opened and the men at the table looked up and the television crowd glanced down.

"Who's makin' a fool of himself? Every time I step off, somebody acts up. What's goin' on?"

Marie stepped in and strolled toward the bar, returning the smiles. She moved as if she were onstage and did not seem at all like the Marie Taylor I remembered from the time when her eye had been shut by the force of James's fist.

She was about forty years old, brown complexion, and medium height but appeared taller in the four-inch heels and hair piled in a sweep of red-brown curls. Her face was heart-shaped and her large eyes gave her a slightly surprised expression. The short brown suede skirt and black suede sleeveless jacket hugged her frame as she moved.

"Hey, Marie," a man in a Mets cap called as she passed. "Gimme some sugar. Ain't seen you in a dog's age."

"Well, your dog still a pup 'cause you seen me just yesterday."

She kissed him anyway and patted him lightly on the shoulder. She moved on and he got a stool, dragged it down to where I sat, and made a show of dusting it off for her.

"See what you get when you good?" he said, winking at her. She kissed him again, shooed him away, and sat down.

"You Miss Anderson, right? Those eyes ain't changed."

"Mali. Yes."

"Good. What're you havin'?" She signaled for the barmaid. "Hey, Shaneeka, Betty here yet?"

Shaneeka, short and small and clad in red spandex from neck to knee, rolled her eyes as she moved toward us. "Now, you know tonight's her birthday. Girlfriend still home gettin' it together. What you havin'?"

"The usual, only colder than last time."

Shaneeka returned with a Miller Lite, tipped Marie's glass until a thin layer of foam blanketed the rim, then placed a small bowl of peanuts in front of us.

"Freshen your drink?" she asked.

"Not right now," I said, tapping my half-filled glass. I intended to sip slow while I drew the story out. Marie waited until the barmaid moved away before she spoke.

"So you tryin' to find out about James." She picked at the few peanuts, popped them delicately in her mouth, then took a sip of beer. "First off, lemme say this. When I hooked up with him, he was already separated from Claudine. I didn't break up nobody's happy home. I want that understood, okay?"

"Okay," I said, wondering what game he had dropped on this one between his GQ styling and bald-faced lying.

James was two years older than Claudine and raised in the 115th Street projects by an aunt who substituted for a permanently absent father and a frequently absent mother. Before alcohol had cut the inroads into his face, he had been a good-looking man. A weak man but good-looking enough to pull a woman in hip-deep before she caught him in his lies, which he explained away with more lies. As he had done with Claudine. And when the lies about his college background and his plans for a law degree eventually cornered him, he'd used his fists to make his way out.

Claudine had come to my door one night with her face swollen so large she couldn't speak. Dad had collared Ruffin and grabbed a baseball bat and gone out looking for him but he'd disappeared. Hit and run . . .

"James, you know, got a way of talkin' his way into things," Marie said. "He gas a woman up, tell her how fine she look, how she so rare. You know, all the stuff a woman want to hear, though deep down, you know the brother's lyin', comin' on wrong, scammin'. All James got is a degree in B.S. and it wasn't long before I found out he didn't have too much of nuthin' else."

She said this as if she'd read my mind. James probably knew his game was weak and his strategy was to move in on a woman fast, dazzle her, and hope she'd remain dazzled. When the glow faded and the questions began, then the violence started.

I nodded and raised my glass, waiting for her to continue.

"So he tried comin' on Rambo a few times. He got real strong arms and he like to come up on you, sneakylike. Come from behind with somethin' in his hand swingin—a stick, a bottle, a belt. Two times he tried that shit with me. You know that 'cause you answered one of the nine-elevens . . ."

I nodded again, remembering running with three other officers down a dim hall in a five-story walkup where a hefty young woman had opened her door and pointed to the apartment near the end of the corridor.

"They at it again," she had said. "That door right there."
Her voice had been strong with anger and flowed over the
blare of her television set.

"I don't know how that girl stand it. I dimed him out and
you can tell him I did. If he base up at me, I'll beat his buns
into the carpet. Tell him I said that too!"

The light streaming from behind her had accented the
sweat on her narrow nose. She was really not that big a
woman but her hands on her hips were balled into fists the
size of large, unripe avocados and she was prepared to back
up her conversation.

I imagined a set of hundred-pound barbells propped in
front of her living room television and a library of workout
tapes.

"We'll handle it, miss," I said, thankful we hadn't been
called to *her* apartment. "Thanks for calling."

Marie sipped her beer now, remembering also. "He tried
that shit twice, and after that, I said three strikes, mother-
fucker's out. So one night, I'm standin' at the stove and he
come up talkin' some stuff about how the fish ain't fried crisp
enough. Here I am tryin' to get things together fast, done
worked a double while he home all day chillin' with Montel
and Rolling Rock . . ."

"He wasn't working?"

"He was supposed to be workin' but he had got suspended for a few days."

"Why?"

"Harassin' some girl, so he said."

"What did he do?"

"I didn't get the full story 'cause we wasn't on the same shift, and when I asked him, he went tight—said somebody had set him up. And it wasn't until two weeks later, I found out the real deal—that he'd been fired. The girl had brought him up on charges, and at the hearing he threatened her in front of the supervisor and the union rep. How stupid can a dumb man get?

"So he home with his feet up lookin' at Montel—you'd think he'd a learned somethin' watchin' the show? I mean, Montel drop some science. He is so *upliftin'*, you know what I mean, even if he is marry to that white woman. He try to up*lift* you, you know?"

I took a long swallow this time, not wanting to distract her with my opinion. I imagined James slouched in front of the television belching loud enough to be heard in the next apartment.

"So what happened?"

"So I'm standin' there and my feet hurtin'—nobody mess with me when my feet is hurtin'—and the fool come at me swingin' a belt. A goddamn belt. My daddy died fifteen years ago and this fool think he gonna step in his spot. Come at me with a damn belt. Tellin' me how to fry fish.

"Well, I turned 'round with that pan and said, 'Fish ain't crisp? How you like some crisp-fried dick, motherfucker?'

"And I'm tellin' you, when that smokin' oil hit, it went right through his pants and I ain't seen dancin' like that since the old James Brown days at the Apollo.

"I probably missed 'cause he wasn't swingin' that much equipment to begin with. Anyway, I booked. Come back next day with the cops to get my stuff.

"Now I got my order of protection right here in my bag. Carry it all the time."

She shook her head and turned sideways to the bar, snapping her fingers in time to early Ray Charles. On the television a baseball player slid soundlessly into third, and the face of the commentator wrinkled with excitement.

Marie ordered another beer and added, almost as an afterthought, "I ain't went in front a no judge neither."

"James didn't press charges?" I said, surprised that he'd let her get away with that.

"I'm not talkin' about no charges. I'm talkin' about my protection. Paper from a judge don't mean diddly. A man get that postal virus, he shoot right through that paper. So I got me somethin' a whole lot better."

She snapped her purse open and in the half-light I caught the dull sheen of the weapon's gray-black, polycarbonate casing.

"Where'd you get a Glock?" I whispered.

"Mine to know and yours to find out," she said, closing the bag, calmer now. "I know one thing, he ain't layin' a hand on me again and he ain't basin' up in my face again neither."

She crossed her legs and balanced the suede bag loosely in her lap, stroking it the way one would smooth the fur of a cat.

"You know, when I came to my senses and really thought

about his situation, I think he was mad and mean all the time 'cause he was kinda—how you say—anatomily—"

"Anatomically?"

"Yeah. I heard that word the other day and had to go look it up. You know, the way they talk about how homeless people is supposed to be 'residentially challenged.' Ain't that some shit? Homeless mean you can't afford these ass-high rents, that's why you out to the curb.

"Well, so like James was 'anatomically challenged.' You know what I'm sayin'? There was a show on TV about that. Some guys talkin' about the operations they had to make their wee willies more wonderful. I tell you, some men spend money on the damnest things."

I closed my eyes and thanked Mother Nature or whoever was responsible for Tad.

"Now, personally," Marie said, "I look at it this way: it ain't the size of the boat, it's how you rockin' it. It's the motion in the ocean. That's what counts."

On the screen the batter had lined to third and the baseman hustled, caught it, and spun around arming it to first. The runner was out, ending the game. The screen went dark and someone notched up the jukebox.

Marie lifted her glass and drained it. Another song came on, but the tune, something called "A Perpetual Blues Machine," was not familiar to me. Marie knew it and hummed along with the deep, cutting rhythm of the harmonica and guitar. I listened, nodding my head absently, and watched her somber reflection in the dimly lit mirror behind the bar.

I was acutely aware of Benin's absence now. If she had been here, Claudine would have confided in her. Claudine had never mentioned to me any physical problems she'd had with James—except that he couldn't keep his hands off other women and couldn't keep his fist out of her face—and she never talked about anything dealing with sex. She had left that to Elizabeth and Deborah and me and rolled her eyes whenever the talk got to be too much for her.

I wondered now why Claudine chose to hang out with us. When we were younger, Deborah was cool but Elizabeth and I had earned several nicknames from our parents: "wild life" and "free spirit" were some of the nicer ones. Elizabeth's father had once threatened to send her to boarding school in Alaska and my dad had threatened to send me to a psychiatrist to try to understand, if not necessarily cure, my wild ways.

Benin and Claudine had been conservative, Deborah was somewhere in between, while Elizabeth and I had been the sisters who knew what life was about. The brothers we attracted had to come with a strong game.

If Benin had been here, perhaps Claudine, gentle and pretty, wouldn't have fallen into the fine web spun by the weak and handsome James:

"Got my applications in for law school," he had boasted. "Post office a temporary thing. Tuition, you know. Ought to hear from Hofstra or Fordham any day now . . ."

They had married quickly and Claudine later found that James had barely squeaked through high school one point past the bottom line of a GED and had later flunked out of three different colleges. Law school had been a dim mirage which receded from his low horizon the minute she'd said, "I do."

"Listen, Mali," Marie said, tapping my hand. "I know James had some problems. He was mean and quick-tempered and fast with his fists, but I don't know. I can't see him actually killin' anybody. I mean, he had plenty reason to come after me 'cause of that hot-oil thing, but he didn't . . ."

"Maybe he knew enough to leave you alone," I said. "Some men will only abuse those who're willing to put up with it. And some women put up and shut up for the sake of love, marriage, or the children. You did what you had to do and walked."

"Ran—"

"Whatever. But before you booked, you left a message he's not likely to forget."

I watched her hand smooth the bag in her lap. It slowed, then moved again in small circles, and I wondered if she was thinking what I was thinking: that James did not forget but was simply waiting for the right moment.

chapter

seven

Two hours later I was ready to leave. The crowd had grown large waiting for the birthday girl and the music had gotten louder. Several drinks were sent our way and Marie had switched to Rémy and was no longer interested in talking about James. She raised her glass, and her smile triggered more drinks, which flowed toward us in a steady stream. I decided to stop at three.

"Listen, Marie, I appreciate you taking the time. If you think of anything else, give me a call."

I gave her my personal card and moved from the stool.

"You sure you don't want to stay? Party's just gettin' started."

"Another time," I said, "and thanks again."

I made my way toward the door. Space was tight, drinks were moving, and conversation was loud. I moved slowly, and a short distance from the door, I recognized a familiar voice. James was leaning into the face of a young woman sitting at the bar.

"Say, beautiful, you don't mind if I call you that since we haven't been formally introduced yet? But you look like a Libra. Am I right?" He was as smooth as Olestra and just as bogus.

The woman looked through him, yawned, and picked up her glass.

James persisted. "Okay, it probably ain't Libra. So, what sign *are* you?"

"Dollar sign," the girl said through teeth so tight it probably pained her.

"Oh," James said, "in that case, lemme go check my ATM." He stretched a grin but stepped back as if she had slapped him.

Before he had a chance to look my way, I turned around and edged through the crowd again to the end of the bar. A tall, dark, powerfully built man with a shaven head was deep in conversation with Marie and she was smiling up at him. She waved. "Say hello to Clyde. He's a coworker, the one sent all the drinks."

He shook my hand. The grip was as strong as he looked and his voice was low bass against the rhythm of the Dells pumping from the jukebox.

"Changed your mind about leavin'? One a my buddies had wanted to talk to you. Said you had the prettiest eyes he ever saw. Brother was hypnotized."

I smiled and shook my head, pulling at Marie's arm. "Another time, okay? I've got to tell Marie something . . ."

He shrugged, disappointed, as Marie slipped from the stool and followed me to the ladies' room.

"Your face lookin' funny. What's up?"

"James is here. At the end of the bar. I thought you should know."

"Shit. I don't need him messin' up my good time. I been tryin' to get next to Clyde for a while now."

"What are you going to do?"

"Well, I ain't leavin', that's for sure. I'm hangin' with Clyde for the duration. James see someone that size, he ain't likely to start no shit. Besides, I got my backup in my bag, remember? But thanks for lookin' out for me."

She touched a comb to her hair and freshened her lipstick and we left the room. I made my way through the crowd again, carefully, trying to spot James. He was gone, probably blown out by the Dollar Sign Sister.

When I stepped outside, a silver stretch had pulled to the curb and the chauffeur raced around the side, shooed the crowd, and opened the door. Betty, the barmaid, stepped out wearing a see-through sheath with clusters of silver sequins that glittered like Fourth of July sparklers when she moved.

She was tall and slim and had a bottle of Cristal cradled in one arm and a bouquet of yellow and red long-stem roses in the other. She spotted me and waved the bouquet.

"Mali, baby, you're not leavin', are you? When will you see a night like this again? I'm celebratin' my half a hundred. Won't see this again. Come on back inside."

"Betty, I'm sorry," I said, wishing I could. The door of the bar popped open, releasing the rhythm of Stevie Wonder like a hot current. Its undertow pulled people inside and I was sorry, truly sorry, that I couldn't stay. "Have to get home. Dad has a gig."

"Club Harlem?"

"Yes. I've got to be home before he leaves."

"Tell 'im to drop by when he finish up, you hear?"

I smiled and waved. "Catch you at the next fifty."

Someone opened the door again and she stepped in, sailed in, to the rhapsody of Stevie Wonder's "Happy Birthday."

The small crowd that had gathered when the limo pulled up followed in her wake. All except James, who had been standing directly behind me. When I turned, I nearly tripped but he did not move. He stared, playing the childish street game of waiting for me to move around him. I knew the rules:

moving around meant backing down. I felt the bile rise at the
back of my throat and did not move but gave him eye for eye.
Up close, his skin was like broken stone and he was wrapped
in the odor of stale alcohol. No wonder the Dollar Sign Sister
had turned away. I imagined vapors strong enough to light a
candle when he'd opened his mouth.

"Step off, James. You know I don't play."

"Neither do I," he whispered. "I peeped what went
down. You talkin' to that bitch in there."

"What bitch? Nobody introduced me to your mama."

He stepped back, his eyes narrowing into one of those
taut Freddy Krueger nightmare stares, and began to circle me.
I stood my ground, feeling my blood pump hard as I went
into a slight crouch. I had on my size 10 hoochie heels, just
out the box, and intended to aim and hit what Marie had
missed with that hot oil.

The standoff might have lasted until the bar closed, but
someone, a cohort in as bad a shape as James, came rushing
out.

"Man, they poppin' free champagne! Free! And they got
free food! What you doin' out here?"

James turned, but before he walked, he whispered,
"When you was on the force, you was big and bad with
backup. It ain't that way no more. You be hearin' from me."

"It's not about the force and you know it, James."

"Whatever. But you'll be hearin' from me."

"And I'll be ready," I called after his retreating back.

chapter

eight

At Malcolm X Boulevard the group of young African women standing in their usual circle at the IRT listened to the subway train pull in. As the doors opened, their chant began, soft, like singing in church. "Evening, madam. Braids, madam? Beautiful braids, right upstairs."

One took a solo as I passed. "Sister. Braids will make you especially more beautiful. Won't you visit our salon?"

I smiled and shook my head. I had neither the nine hours to spare nor the ninety dollars to spend in order to find out. I walked past the Casablanca Bar, the bright and busy lights of Sylvia's, and the takeout line at Majestic's Seafood.

Thin streaks of purple still dotted the western edge of sky and I walked quickly, moving past sad rows of tenements dotted with buildings sealed up and businesses that had given up. Retail shops that had once opened with promise and fanfare and plastic pennants fluttering in a "V" now announced failure, reflected failure, in graffiti-patterned steel shutters.

James receded to the back of my mind as I walked past block after block of desolation, thinking of the empowerment zone. Empowerment dollars. Money and power flying right past lives and buildings crumbling brick by brick onto crumbling sidewalks. Dad had described the sixties' War on Poverty where the warlords stashed the booty and left the poor still waiting for the miracle.

I managed to cool down a bit when I turned into 139th Street, a block of neo-Italian Renaissance and neo-Georgian houses. W. C. Handy, Noble Sissle, and Eubie Blake once lived here, and Dad swears that he feels their spirit in his work. This block of houses, designed by Stanford White in 1891, had been nicknamed Strivers' Row because of the number of black professionals who bought homes here.

I composed myself before I put the key in the door, but when I walked in, Alvin, my not-quite-teenage nephew, glanced up from the television, then stared at me.

"Who'd you run into? From the look on your face, if you'd been driving, there'd've been nothing left to scrape up, but here you doin' road rage on foot."

I preferred not to answer. Getting the last word on James by calling up his mama was low. The poor woman was probably as disappointed in him as everyone else was.

And Dad once said that back in the day, some folks died from "playing the dozens." Some got killed on the spot and he knew of one who had managed to do himself in: a young guitar player in a traveling band who had ascribed the b-word to his girlfriend so often, eventually they both forgot her real name. Her memory resurrected quicker than his, and when he came in from a trip one time, he spent three days studying the good-bye note bannered with her real signature. They found him in the bathroom, his head between his knees and the "works," flushed pink with blood, still in his arm.

James got the message that I was not playing. The b-word, like the n-word, was off the rim, and I had to make it plain. Now I drew a deep breath, determined to forget about him, at least for now.

"Where's Dad?" I said.

"Downstairs gettin' ready."

I opened the door leading down to his studio, and the muted strains of Miles Davis's "Blues by Five" floated up. A minute later Dad came upstairs, resplendent in a white dinner jacket and black trousers.

"You look like a million," I said. "And, speaking of millions, I just saw Betty stepping out a stretch at the Lido. Tonight's her birthday. She wants you to stop by after your gig."

Dad ran his hand over his close-cut hair—salt and pepper against dark brown skin. His features were regular, and despite years of bass playing in clubs and after-hours spots with cigarette smoke dense enough to require a respirator, his skin was still unlined and he still walked with the sure step of a man much younger than sixty-two.

"Hey." He was smiling at the idea of going from one party to another, like the old days. "Maybe I pull some of the guys. Four A.M. we break in like Western Union, a singin' telegram. She'll like that."

He paused and looked at me narrowly. "What were you doin' around the Lido? I thought you had headed to the Schomburg earlier to do some research?"

"Dad, really. That's what I intended, but I got detoured and—"

"Mali, your classes begin in less than two months. You don't want to—"

"No, Dad. I can promise you right now, I plan to pass those exams and then develop the best dissertation NYU has ever seen."

The horn of a waiting car rescued me. But I heard a sigh as he shrugged, grabbed his bass, and angled it out the door. "See you all later. Remember what I said about that television, Alvin. By ten-thirty I want you lookin' at the inside of your eyelids."

"Yes, sir." Alvin drew his legs up under him, his eyes glued to the choreography of four three-hundred-pound tag team wrestlers bouncing past each other. The hardest thing they seemed to hit was the canvas, with much howling and leaping and palm pounding. I sat down next to Alvin but five minutes of bogus bumping and ricocheting was all I could take.

"What do you get out of this?" I asked, wondering if I could develop his reply into a dissertation on the need to accept outright fraud and call it entertainment.

Alvin shrugged. "I don't know. Guys are bogus but got some dope shifts. I might learn something."

I abandoned the sofa for the quiet of my room but I couldn't relax. James was like a bad taste on my tongue; a pinprick on my skin whose irritation had spread in a poisonous current and was infecting other parts of me.

I sat at my desk and pored over my small notebook. A half dozen pages were filled and I added a few more, including a note on the weapon Marie carried. I read again the condition of Claudine's body when she had been found. The fact that nothing had been stolen. The time Elizabeth had last spoken to her. Then I underlined in red James's remark outside the Lido.

I turned back to page one and gazed at the date of Claudine's death and thought about the unfixable grief of her parents. It had been nearly five weeks. Too much time was passing without answers. I thought of Marie again. As much as James had abused her, she didn't think he was capable of murder. Why then was she hugging that Glock?

chapter

nine

He didn't like the way the voices sounded lately. Loud, insistent to the point where turning up his Walkman to blast level wasn't helping. One voice in particular he couldn't tolerate, couldn't even breathe when he heard it. Sounded too much like his mama.

It *was* his mama.

Hazel was screaming, reminding him for the thousandth time how she'd been in labor for sixty-eight straight hours just so his worthless ass could see the light of day:

Begged that fuckin' doctor to crush your skull, fold it in so your worthless ass could just shoot out of me.

And the doctor said, "You're confused, Mother. You don't mean what you're saying." And I told 'im, "Fuck you, mother-fucker, and don't call me 'Mother.' You ain't nuthin' to me, understand?"

And you know what that doctor did?

Ache breathed deeply, knowing the answer, heard it so many times he'd memorized it.

He said, "Maybe you shoulda lost some a that weight before you decided to become pregnant. Being overweight is dangerous, Mother. Could cause complications. See you in a few hours."

And he walked out and shut the door, just like your no-good daddy, that goddamn son of a bitch.

Well, here you come a whole goddamn two days later, not just some fuckin' few hours. And everybody looked, said you was ugly as hell. Still ugly. Shoulda put your head in the toilet minute I got home.

Twenty years ago, when he was younger, they didn't have Walkmans, and even if they did, he couldn't have afforded one. But at times he managed to place a small cardboard box over his head and blow in it, made sounds like the wind rushing in his ears while his mother cursed him outside the bathroom door where he'd locked himself.

In school, where he couldn't take the box, the jabs came at him like heat-seeking missiles riding waves of sniggering. Even the teacher—who hid her face at the board but couldn't quite control her shaking shoulders—did nothing when that worn-out Redd Foxx joke broke over the class.

"You was so ugly when you was born, the doc went and slapped your mama."

Worn-out. Old. But powerful enough to cause burning injury. Funny enough for the girls to laugh if the right boy told it. They laughed. The boys were stupid, but the girls, they should've known better. So that made them extra-stupid. Just like his mama. They should've known better.

The doc slapped yo' mama. *Aaaaargh!*

And his mama, in turn, had never stopped slapping him. Words. The sharp heel of a shoe, the ironing cord, the iron itself, the key enclosing him in a closet so dark that even the flashing light inside his head went out.

And that cereal. Spread all over the floor.

The pounding shook him, made him jump. He looked around the small bedroom, confused. Was the sound coming from outside? Inside? There it was again, like a hammer.

He snatched the earphones away, listening in the dark. There was a silence, then something like static, like he'd turned to a bad station in Minnesota. A jangle of voices again and finally that dominant one:

What you waitin' for, Ache? You saw the way she looked at you. Disrespected you. You don't have to take that shit from nobody. Nobody, you know what I'm sayin'?

He managed to close his eyes.

Yesterday had been bad. The air-conditioning had broken down in the store again and he'd struggled in the heat to stock the shelves and pack the groceries as quickly as he could while that asshole manager was climbin' all over him.

Tellin' me I wasn't hustlin' fast enough. Shit. Why the fuck didn't he pitch in instead of mouthin' off?

Then that woman. Movin' down the aisle like she the point tank for fuckin' Desert Storm. That tight suede skirt. And snatchin' stuff and swingin' that shoulder bag like she had a .45 in it. And starin' at me like I was a piece a shit.

The noise faded, gave way to other sounds. Floorboards creaked under his mother's weight and he lay against the pillows, exhausted, waiting for the door to fly open again and the air to ring hot with her howling for at least another hour.

When the door slammed open, the inside voice spiraled up again, up and over his mother's screaming.

What you waitin' for, Ache? the voice inside said. *You saw how the bitch eyed you. And you know, you be on the news again. Not just WINS, but TV this time. You be on top of the world. You know how O.J. stopped the stock market? The fuckin' stock market! Hell, they could do that for you . . .*

chapter

ten

A storm passed through during the night, waking me. By dawn, the few inches of rain had already evaporated into the parched pavement and I knew we were facing another ninety-degree day.

I lay in bed, listening to the undulating wail of an ambulance, then the blast of a fire engine racing to some distant catastrophe; a few doors away a car maneuvered from a parking spot and moved on a whisk of tires down the street into silence.

Five A.M. An hour before the day actually intruded, before time to shower, walk Ruffin, and before Dad and Alvin stirred. After some research at the Schomburg on early black social work organizations, I wanted to call Deborah to find out how she was feeling; visit Claudine's parents even though I had nothing new to tell them. Call Elizabeth. Perhaps she'd want to come with me.

The sound of the phone cut into my reverie.

"Mali. You awake?"

"I am now," I said, easing to sit up straight. Tad came on sounding as if he'd been up all night and he wasn't calling to tell me how much he missed me.

"What . . . what's going on?"

The slight hesitation let me know bad news was coming.

"It's Marie," he whispered.

"Marie? What happened?"

"She was found in her apartment around one A.M. Door was ajar and a neighbor pushed it but was afraid to go in. Thought robbers were inside. The neighbor ran back to her own place and called in a nine-eleven. It's a good thing she didn't go in."

"Was it a break-in? Were the perps still in there?"

"No."

"What, then?"

"She was killed the same way Claudine was. Wire."

My stomach contracted. Marie. She'd had the gun. She'd been prepared. How had someone slipped past?

"Mali? You still there?"

"Yes. Barely."

"We got a net out for James but he's gone up in smoke. It'll be in the *Daily Challenge* this morning, that's why I wanted to let you know. Before you read about it. Anything breaks, I'll call right away."

The phone went dead and I stared at the receiver in my hands, waiting for more information to spill into the silence.

. . . Wire. Like Claudine. And James has disappeared.

It was hard not to fold up and crawl back under the sheets, shut my eyes, and shut down my brain.

Marie had been prepared to fight, to pull that piece at the slightest provocation. How had this happened?

I kicked the covers away and padded to the bathroom to stand under the shower until the stinging-cold water beat me fully awake.

"I'll tell you something," Dad said as he folded the *Daily Challenge* flat on the dining table. I had opened the door as soon as the paper had been delivered along with the rest of the mail. I was hoping that Tad had been wrong but the lead story stared me in the face.

Now Dad was reading it. "You know, James really showed his colors the other night in the Lido," he said. "No wonder the cops are looking for him."

My throat went dry and I put my cup down. "At the

Lido? You never said anything had happened that night. You said everyone had had a good time and Betty'd been happy that you showed."

I watched Dad refill his cup. The breaking sun slanted in through the window and chased the earlier gray, revealing his face in frowning profile.

"I kept quiet 'cause I know how you feel about James and how he treated Claudine," he said. "Claudine's gone and James is still here and it seems a leopard don't never change his spots.

"When me and the fellas popped in, the Lido was in full swing. We stepped in, tuned up just like I planned, then made our way to the back and was settin' up on the bandstand when we hear this noise, this loud crash up front near the door. A table was overturned and there was James, doin' a '60 Minutes' profile. Except when he opened his mouth, I thought a toilet had backed up. Every other syllable was 'f' and 'n' and 'b.'

"Finally this woman"—he tapped Marie's photo on the front page—"I guess all that language was aimed at her. Anyway, she left her barstool, walked up the front, and read him out. Told him and the whole bar how he wasn't even a man, 'cause a real man would be about a man's business, not about wastin' time cursin' and makin' a fool of himself.

"He started for her, and this big, clean head brother just come out the men's room, stepped up. Plus four guys, old as me, sitting at a table, cleared that railing like Olympic high jumpers. Moved like athletes. Next thing I knew, James was out the door and huggin' up the recyclin' can at the curb.

"We cut into a jam and things snapped back. Drinks flowed and folks started partyin' again.

"Betty told me later that James had been actin' crazy from the jump, thought maybe he'd run into some static on the street and his attitude rode in when he stepped through the door. Who knows? Anyway, they evicted him for steppin' up to this girl."

He gazed at the picture. "Damn shame," he whispered. "A damn shame. This girl's dead."

I stared at the table with the platters of pancakes, bacon, fresh strawberries, and scrambled eggs. Alvin was late getting up and now I heard the shower running and his voice singing above the noise. I wanted to get up and take the platters back to the kitchen, to keep them warm until he came down, but I could not move.

I was the person who'd confronted James that night, caused him to get an attitude. Why didn't he come after me? Instead he'd gone after his ex-girlfriend.

I collared Ruffin and left the house, heading for St. Nicholas Park, avoiding Edgecombe Avenue because I did not want to look up at the curtainless windows of Claudine's empty apartment.

The stairs through the park led up to St. Nicholas Terrace winding behind City University. The grass smelled fresh and a light sprinkle of rainwater still dropped from the leaves when the wind disturbed them.

From the terrace, I gazed down over the steep incline of the park and the playground. A bus moved busily along St. Nicholas Avenue, discharging passengers, taking in more, and moving on. Purposefully. Everyone on that bus had a destination. Even the driver had a purpose. To get where he had to go, complete the assigned route.

I turned around to face the Gothic mass of Shepherd Hall, my favorite building on the campus. Students were already in class, poring, just as I once had, over their assignments. With purpose.

"I'm going to find James," I said.

I spoke to Ruffin because there was no one else to make this promise to. Ruffin looked up, then rested his head on the ground between his paws. Two campus security guards watched us from a safe distance across the street, reluctant to approach. They stared at Ruffin and I let a minute pass before I waved good morning. One lifted his hand halfheartedly, as if he feared Ruffin would leap across the street and snack on his arm for breakfast.

"Come on, Ruffin. The guys are getting nervous."

We left the winding walk at 140th Street and came out on Convent Avenue, passing the John Henrik Clarke House, a brownstone named for one of the founders of the Harlem

Writers Guild. At Convent Avenue Baptist Church we turned east and walked down the hill at 145th Street, weaving our way through the crowd rushing to the subway.

Dad said that when Florence Mills, a popular entertainer in the 1920s, died, the funeral procession had moved down this street and 100,000 people had lined the sidewalk watching in silence as a low-flying plane released a huge flock of blackbirds.

"They don't have send-offs like that anymore," he complained, but I reminded him of James Baldwin's funeral: how Olatunji's Drums of Passion had echoed against the vaulted stone of the Cathedral of St. John the Divine and how the dancers, dressed in elaborate flowing white pantaloons, pranced and somersaulted down the aisles to the sound of the drums. The ceremony had ended with thousands of candles held aloft and there wasn't a dry eye in the place. That was a send-off that I remembered.

On St. Nicholas Avenue I walked past the Bowery Building apartments where Dinah Washington had lived, then I slowed at Malcolm X Boulevard. I began to peek at darkened doorways, cellar entrances, steps leading down to doors below the stoops of sealed houses. If I spotted James, the police could have what was left of him.

"Hey, hey. Good mornin', Mali."

I turned around, pulling Ruffin up short. "Dr. De. Good morning. Sorry I didn't see you."

"Yeah well, I see you, and from the look on your face, I

don't know who you after, but I wouldn't wanna be it. Between you and the horse, I wouldn't stand a chance . . ."

Dr. De owned Creative Cuts and was known for correcting the serious mistakes other barbers had made. His technique was so precise that he'd earned the title of doctor of tonsorial arts, and the weekends saw standing-room-only in his place.

I started going to Creative Cuts after the Klip Joint on 116th Street had closed. Between Dr. De and Bertha, the hairdresser I visited for deep conditioning and light gossip, I managed to keep my hair in shape.

Dr. De had been sweeping in front of the shop and paused to lean on his broom. "Look, Mali. I know how you're feelin' about Claudine but believe me, time'll take care of things."

I did not mention the latest killing but continued to glance up and down the avenue.

"How's everything else?" he said, changing the subject and eyeing my hair. "Can't let yourself fall apart, you know. The beat goes on whether we like it or not and we got to keep steppin' to it."

I nodded but still could not reply. I was aware that I hadn't had a haircut in nearly a month. I mean I couldn't exactly challenge Rapunzel, but Dr. De was responsible for keeping the growth I had somewhat under control. Lately I'd convinced myself that a quick shampoo under the shower was enough to get me through the day. I hadn't even stopped in to say hello to Bertha at her shop. I told myself that I had too many other things to think about, but the reality was that I couldn't shake the grief that had wound its way inside, gnawing at me.

I stopped glancing around long enough to focus on Dr. De, a young man with a handsome face and round glasses set on the edge of his thin nose. His short beard and knit kufi gave him a scholarly appearance. Most barbershops had magazines and newspapers lying around but Dr. De had books.

"I'll be in soon," I said. "I . . . have to—get myself together."

"I hear you. You take it easy. Things'll work out."

He probably wanted to step up and hug me but he glanced again at Ruffin and thought better of it. "Things'll work out," he said again.

chapter

eleven

By the time I reached home, the constriction in my throat had not completely disappeared but I was able to breathe a little easier. Alvin was in his room, chatting on the Internet, and I could hear faint notes from Dad in the studio downstairs.

On my night table, the message light was blinking, and Tad's voice filled the room when I pressed the button.

"Hi, baby. It's ten o'clock. If you get this message within the hour, I'll be in Wells Restaurant till noon. Let's have chicken and waffles or a cup of coffee. Or both. I love you."

I changed from my sweats and put on a pair of silk slacks and a cotton top. Before I left again, I peeped in on Alvin. He was hunched in concentration in front of his PC, holding the mouse as if it were the key to lost treasure. He glanced up and smiled.

"I know. I know," he said, holding out his free hand. "Five more minutes, then I log off. Grandpa doesn't want me to spend the entire summer on this thing. Says it leads to social isolation. But I'm not isolated. I can connect with people in Africa, Japan, Australia, Germany. All over the world."

Before I could open my mouth, he knew what I was going to say, knew I agreed with Dad, so he glanced quickly at his watch and cut me off at the pass. "Uh-oh. He's waitin' for me now. Bass."

He turned the machine off. Bass practice for two hours. Dad was teaching him, a day at a time, everything he himself had ever learned about music. I worried that the computer was becoming serious competition and was glad when Dad put his foot down.

"Boy! Unless you're on dialysis," he had said, "there's no reason to be hooked to a machine for so many hours. Two hours is enough for any sane person to sit in front of a blinking screen. I don't care if you're able to access the winning lottery number from it. Enough is enough."

"What are you doing after practice?" I asked, knowing that he couldn't go back to the computer.

"Basketball. Morris called while you were out. I'm gonna meet him and Clarence at the court."

. . . Thank God. Let him get the exercise. Feel some sweat. Talk and yell and laugh with real people.

I nodded, somewhat mollified, and left the house again.

The rebirth of Wells Restaurant on Adam Clayton Powell Jr. Boulevard near 132nd Street added to the number of trend-setting restaurants in the area. Of course, most folks still remembered the original Wells that catered to the 3:00 A.M. crowds when the dance halls—the Savoy, the Rennie, the Audubon, the Park Palace, and Rockland Palace—emptied out and the true night owls who wouldn't dream of going home without fueling up on a platter of chicken and waffles.

From its opening in 1938 and before it closed in 1982, Pearl Bailey, Aretha Franklin, Jackie Robinson, Frank Sinatra, and any politician worth a vote had visited Wells at least once.

Joe Wells died in 1987, and in 1992 his widow reopened the place. The dance halls are a memory but the Monday night big-band sessions and Sunday brunches pull a respectable number.

I walked past the bar and into the large dining room where Tad was sitting at a table gazing out at Seventh Avenue. I slid into the seat opposite him and he leaned over to brush his fingers near my ear. His face looked as if he'd just come off a rendezvous with a bad dentist.

"Sorry I had to give you more bad news. How you doin', baby?"

"Not too good," I whispered. "Any word on James?"

"No, but I got a call about an hour ago. Buddy of mine works homicide in the Four-Eight. Said there was a similar situation in the Bronx a few years ago. Three murders within a ten-block radius. There was the wire, cereal, no forced entry or prints, but some fibers were picked up from the back of the women's clothing. They came from a dark brown jogging suit. From there, the case went cold. He's sending me samples for a matchup. Also, all the murders took place within six weeks and then stopped. The women were killed on Thursdays, early to midevening. Same M.O."

"So what are you thinking?"

He continued to gaze out of the window, frowning. His eyes were deep-set and his pupils appeared to take on the intense gold of the sunlight spilling into the room. He moved his hand to send his fingers through his close-cut, silver-edged hair, and I caught myself drifting away from the nightmare and easing into something warm, lush, and licentious.

"I'm thinking," Tad said, quietly bringing me back, "that either the guy got busted for something else that maybe took him off the street for a while, or he skipped one step ahead of the net and decided to lay low until the urge hit him again.

"We're loading everything into the computer to check the in and out dates of known violent offenders."

"Does this let James off the hook?"

"Not hardly. I want to know about—"

A small ring interrupted and he flipped his cell phone. His

expression hardened and he rose from the table, snapping the phone off.

"I'll let you know about James in an hour. Maybe less," he whispered. "He's at the precinct. They just brought him in."

We skipped the chicken and waffles and I returned home to lie across the bed and stare at the play of light and shadows on the ceiling. Dad and Alvin were practicing and bass notes and piano filtered through the quiet. I breathed hard, listening to the pump of my heart, gazing at the rise of my chest, counting a number with each rise. At one hundred, I switched to the alphabet and breathed deeper. Perspiration—or was it tears?—slid down the side of my face, trickling into my ear before settling into a blot on the pillow.

. . . Why doesn't Tad call! It's been over an hour. A whole hour, dammit!

I closed my eyes and imagined James seated at the far end of the table in the interview room at the precinct. Wiping his face, shaking his head as more sweat gathered. I saw his stone-broken face and heard the whiny voice afloat on the thick air in the room. ". . . don't know nuthin', ain't done nuthin', ain't seen nuthin'."

The sound filled me with an unmanageable anger and I found myself wishing I were back in uniform, in that room,

on my way to becoming that thing people hate most in a bad
cop.

I thought of Argentina and Chile where interrogators
broke bones and pulled teeth and tongues and fingernails
without passion or purpose. And wondered what Tad and the
other detectives were doing. But I knew the video was on, the
tape recorder was on. And James was safe, unafraid, and
maybe even a little arrogant behind the veil of his noisy whin-
ing.

Tad was present, so James was assured, after all was said
and done and he'd escaped the death penalty, that he'd walk
into state prison with all his toes and fingers and brains intact.
If he escaped the death penalty.

I rolled over on the pillow and looked at the circles left by
my tears. The circles felt cold and I moved away from them.
The ceiling shadows blurred again as the phone rang and sent
a current of shock to my arm, then to my chest. But it was the
message, not the instrument.

Tad's voice was tight with frustration.

"He had been in Bellevue, Mali. Alcoholic ward. He was
in restraints with that pink elephant kicking his ass the whole
time. Before, during, and after Marie's murder. They cut him
loose this morning and the stakeout collared him when he got
home. He was sober and cried like a baby when we told
'im . . ."

"Bellevue?"

"Yeah. We had to cut him loose. He's not the one. So he
had to walk."

Tad probably said "good-bye" or "so long" or something but I couldn't hear it. A roar had packed the space between the phone and my ear and I lay back on the bed.

Sometime later, a minute perhaps, Dad and Alvin were in the room, bending over me. Alvin shook me and Dad was squeezing my hands. Alvin's face was misshapen by fright.

"What happened? You were screamin'. What . . . what's the matter?"

I stared at them. I didn't know. I couldn't answer.

chapter

twelve

I sent flowers but did not attend Marie's funeral. After Claudine, this was just too much for me. Two days after, I went back to the Lido. The mood was different when I stepped in, although the crowd was the same. The four retirees were at their usual table, nursing bottles of beer and bent in silent concentration over a chessboard. When I walked in, they tipped their caps but the gesture was perfunctory, polite, and their eyes had lost whatever was there when they had glanced at Marie.

Despite the hum of the air conditioner, the atmosphere seemed close, made more melancholy by Gladys Knight's "Midnight Train to Georgia" flowing in a current of remorse from the jukebox.

I took a seat near the front and waited as Betty poured a gin and tonic for a customer seated at the other end. Then she moved toward me and rested her arms on the bar. "How you doin', Mali?"

Before I could answer, she shook her head. "Girl, ain't this some terrible stuff happenin'? Marie. I can't believe that girl is gone."

I nodded, and although it was only three o'clock, too early in the day to be drinking, ordered an Absolut on the rocks. "I wanted to go to the service," I said, "but after Claudine, I just couldn't handle it."

"Don't feel bad." She reached over and touched my arm. "I know how it is. Too much get dumped on you at one time, you don't know whether to face it or fold. Life's a bitch sometimes. But I can say this: she had a big, beautiful sendoff. All her coworkers were there. And Clyde sent a blanket of roses. A blanket. And oh, did he cry! You know how they say some love is strong enough to move heaven and earth? Well, Clyde was strong enough to move earth, but heaven had the last word. Now see, he had eyes for her for years and he was the one she shoulda hooked up with in the first place. Not that low-down James. Now, just as she and Clyde was about to get together, she gets killed. That was no time to die. Girl hardly had a chance to live."

I lifted my glass and thought of Claudine, who was just getting her life back together. It was no time for her to die either.

"And as for James, he didn't even show. Probably too embarrassed at the way he came off at the party. Man is a complete fool. How she put up with him longer than one day is beyond me. I always say a woman can do bad by herself."

I didn't mention that one jug too many of Gypsy Rose had James laid up in a fog at Bellevue. Instead I said, "Has he been in here since she—"

"Hell no. Not after the way he mouthed off, he better not show his face in this place."

She leaned over the bar, lowering her voice. "And I'll tell you this, Mali. I heard through the vine—one of his drinkin' buddies was in here the other night—he was sayin' that James is goin' 'round blamin' you for interfering in his business. Said you turned Claudine against him and that's why she left."

"What?"

"And that ain't all. Said he saw you talkin' to Marie the night of the party and you musta told her somethin' about him. So you watch your back, girl. He is sneaky and he's crazy. Bad combination."

Two men came in and she moved away to take their order. Aretha Franklin's burning voice filtered from the jukebox now, a praise song for feeling like a natural woman. When the tribute ended, I listened in the short silence to the tap of the chess pieces at the retirees' table and wondered what their

days would be like without the presence of Marie, or someone like her, whose young and easy smile helped make them
forget the injury of growing old.

"Where does James live now?" I asked when Betty returned to perch on a stool near the register. The two men had
bought her a brandy and she brought the small glass to her
mouth before she spoke.

"Last place I heard was a rooming house on 136th Street,
couple doors off Malcolm X Boulevard, but he's probably
long gone from there now. You ain't goin' lookin' for him, are
you?"

"Not particularly, but it's always good to know where the
enemy is hiding."

. . . And also to find out why he's spreading these lies. I
had never interfered between him and Claudine. I'd never
mentioned a thing, especially about the incident on her wedding day. I was willing to let sleeping dogs lie, but this lying
dog has to be straightened out.

"Well," Betty sighed, "I'm hoping that they catch whoever did this. I mean I heard she wasn't even robbed. Just
murdered. Nothing was taken from the apartment."

"That's strange," I said, waiting to hear what else might
be on the vine. If anything was there, Betty would know, but
she only shrugged and finished her drink. I finished mine and
paid my check but she pushed the money back at me as I rose
from the stool.

"Listen, Mali." She leaned over now. "You be cool.

Watch your back. Your dad'll be no more good if something happens to you. He already lost one daughter. This ain't no time for you to die. You still got your sister's kid to raise."

"You're right, Betty. I'll remember."

It was a little after four, and the afternoon sky was a cloudless pale blue. I went across the street and joined the waiting line outside Georgie's Bakery and bought a dozen of the donuts that folks would mug you for. Then I walked toward Malcolm X Boulevard, again passing the chorus of African hair braiders with their flowing colors and accents, calling to the sisters to visit their salon.

At 127th Street I called Tad. "How about a walk down near the lake?"

"Baby, you sound out of it. You all right?"

"I'm okay," I said. "I just . . . need to talk."

He was there in ten minutes, and twenty minutes later we were strolling down 110th Street heading for the Fifth Avenue entrance to the Central Park lake, devouring the donuts. But instead of the quiet talk I'd planned, I found myself trying to figure different angles, arguing.

"James is schizoid," I said. "He's not particularly bright but he's cunning. Who's to say he didn't slip out or talk his way out of the hospital and make it back before bed check? Who's to say he wasn't faking when he went in there in the first place? Two women involved with the same man and killed the same way? It can't be anyone else but James."

"No ifs, ands, or buts, Mali. James is not it. You can't pin a rap on someone just because you hate his guts."

"Too bad," I said, wondering how he'd react if he knew how James felt about me. When James had walked away in front of the Lido, he said he would see me again, and sooner or later I knew he was going to keep his promise.

We continued to walk. The pale blue disappeared in the shadows of early evening and the sky turned almost crimson, bathing the walkers, runners, skaters, and cyclists in a singular red cast. As we approached the park, the lake, resembling a large jewel, beckoned us. I wanted to gaze at the water and recall some calming mantra that would help me sort through my feelings.

But Tad stopped suddenly and turned to face me. "Listen, Mali. You're angry and don't know where to direct it. I—"

"Well, what did you expect?" I cried. "Of course I'm angry. I'm damn mad and—"

"And you're not gonna take it anymore. Right? So here's what we're gonna do." He took my arm and we walked past the Duke Ellington monument at the Fifth Avenue circle. The huge piano appeared to float above the elongated arms of the Muses and cast a crisscross of shadow lines on the sidewalk. Inside the park, all the benches were filled, so we sat on the grass at the edge of the lake.

"You've got to make an effort," he said quietly. "An effort to be objective. Get over the idea that it was James. I know what he did to Claudine. He did terrible things but he did not kill her."

"How do you know? How can you be so damn sure?"

My high voice caused people sitting nearby to glance at us. Tad looked out across the lake and let a minute pass. "Lack of evidence," he finally said. "It's just not there, Mali. That's what you have to go by, not your emotion. No matter how much you dislike him, feelings don't count in a court of law."

I remained quiet but inside I was boiling with an anger I knew was irrational.

"Let's look at this from another angle," he said. "There was no money, jewelry, or other property taken, so it wasn't robbery. The guy is probably a psycho, just as you said, but there were no prints or semen to trace. So maybe we should focus on what might have triggered him.

"Claudine and Marie were killed on Thursdays—like the women in the Bronx. It wasn't a copycat because the Bronx details were never publicized. So it's most likely the same person.

"What is it that happens on Thursdays? Or Wednesday nights for that matter? Is the moon full? Is there an electrical storm? Does he run out of medication at that particular time? And the ten-block radius in the Bronx. Was it random or was there something within those blocks that the women might have had in common? Did he live or work there or did he prowl the area looking for likely victims? What's driving him?''

I thought of John Wayne Gacy, Ted Bundy, Son of Sam, Jeffrey Dahmer, and a chill went through me. "You think we have a serial killer loose in Harlem?''

He leaned forward and lowered his voice. "Anything's possible, though we don't get many black serial killers.''

"What about Atlanta in the seventies and eighties?''

"They only convicted Williams for one of those murders and I have my doubts about that one.''

He fell silent again and gazed out at the lake. Across the water, children were launching small sailboats, guiding them by remote control. Their laughter wafted toward us as some of the boats collided. A few minutes passed before Tad spoke: "In any event, Mali, from now on, I'm gonna do this investigation solo. You're still grieving and it's making you crazy.''

"What do you mean by solo," I asked, ignoring everything else he'd said.

"Just what I said. It'd be better if you weren't so involved. You're too close to this . . . this . . .''

I gazed hard at the toy boats and the children. I thought of Claudine and Marie and the life that had been taken from them. They'd had no chance to feel the love of their own child, no chance to watch it grow and sail toy boats.

Despite Tad's argument, I still believed James did it, had taken all of this from Claudine and Marie, and I intended to find him, with or without help.

Tad was still searching for the right word and I didn't wait for him to find it. I got to my feet and walked out of the park without a backward glance.

I strolled uptown, and by the time I'd walked past the Lenox Lounge near 125th Street, I'd made up my mind to look for James. He was sneaky and crazy. He'd come up on Marie from behind to beat her. And I knew all too well what he'd done to Claudine. Now they were dead. I intended to let him know that if he was looking for me, he was looking for trouble and I was ready to meet him face-to-face.

Between Malcolm X and Powell Boulevards, 136th Street was lined with three-story row houses—brick, lime, and brownstone—and anchored by the Countee Cullen Library near Malcolm X and a community center near Powell. Most of the houses were occupied and many others were sealed. One had been abandoned for so long a tree was growing inside. Others had been converted into funeral establishments, small churches, and rooming houses.

A long time ago, my mother had said, "Learn to look at the bells. Five bells or more in a three-story house usually means its a rooming house. Not always, but most of the time."

I counted the bells at a house next door to a sealed building and hit a jackpot of sorts when I pressed the bottom one. It chimed like a church bell and a thin, brown, middle-aged woman in black linen slacks and a yellow cotton pullover appeared at the wrought-iron gate and eyed me carefully before she opened it. A curly wig slanted over her left eye and an unlit cigarette hung from the corner of her mouth and bobbed up and down as she spoke.

"You lookin' for who?"

"James. James Thomas," I repeated.

"Where you from?"

I didn't know if she meant which city, state, or finance company, so I said, "I'm a friend. I was told he—"

She removed the cigarette and rested her hand against the door frame. "Who you foolin', girl? Did Maxie send you?"

"Maxie?"

"From the number hole."

I knew of Maxie from my days on the force. A young Jamaican who sported long silken dreadlocks and who was into loan-sharking, numbers, and a whole lot of other stuff. Rumor had it that he was a man of extremes: loyal to friends, generous with strangers, and vicious with anyone who crossed him. I nodded and shrugged.

"I heard of him but I don't know Maxie personally."

She brushed her hair back from her eyes and looked at me even closer now. And smiled. "You ever go to the Club Harlem? On Fridays? Somehow you look kinda familiar."

"I'm there on Fridays, some Saturdays, and even some Tuesdays," I said. "My dad's group plays—"

"Jeffrey Anderson? He's your father? Well I'll be! Girl, you come on in. We gotta talk. And you don't have to bullshit me to find James. You don't even look like a friend of his, but he probably scammed you too."

She leaned against the gate to unlock it, then swung it open for me to step in. She was comfortable now, and eager for conversation.

"Everybody calls me 'Miss Dottie,' " she said after I had introduced myself. I followed her up a carpeted flight of steps and into a large front parlor. The room was well furnished with old art deco pieces, and a lemon wax fragrance hung in the air. A wing chair with matching footstool faced an enormous marble fireplace flanked by glass-enclosed bookcases. A settee covered in crewel and edged in carved wood was near the window, and a pair of old-fashioned torchieres sent a soft light over the oak wainscoting.

"This is a gas fireplace," she said when she noticed my stare. "Rooms are large, but come winter, these units heat up the rooms faster and better than a log fire."

She motioned me to a seat. "Be right back. Would you like a soda or something?" And without waiting for an answer, disappeared back down the stairs—presumably to the kitchen. This gave me the chance to really look around and admire the Aubusson carpet, the window curtains made of old lace—fine and fragile—and a chandelier dripping crystal-covered lights.

I listened to the slam of a cabinet door, then her footsteps on the stairs again. She placed a black-lacquered tray with two glasses and a large bottle of ginger ale on the table.

"This is quite a place you have. The furnishings are exquisite."

"Thanks. I don't have much company since my husband
passed, but those who visit, especially for the first time, are
always surprised, because the outside looks so shabby. Well, I
ain't dumb. All these pieces was left to me by my folks and I
don't want a stick to walk. Fix up the outside, people think
you doing good inside. Must have somethin' worth breakin' in
for.

"Plenty homes on this block just like mine but we don't
advertise. Right down the block where the Countee Cullen
Library stands is where Madam C. J. Walker had her town
house and next door was her beauty salon. Right there at
number 108 and 110. The town house was named the Dark
Tower, and poetry by Countee Cullen and Langston Hughes
was scripted right on the walls. And she had that fabulous
mansion designed and built in Irvington-on-Hudson by New
York City's first certified black architect. Imagine Madam
C.J., a black lady, doin' all that. And startin' out with only
$1.25 in her pocket and becoming the first self-made female
millionaire, black or white, in this man's country?

"I mean this block has history. What some of us are tryin'
to do now is pressure the city to sell these sealed buildings.
Couple of 'em already been broken into and no tellin' what's
behind those walls. I think about one a them catchin' fire and
spreadin', you know, like they did in Philly. You remember
the MOVE people, how the cops had 'em surrounded and

dropped that bomb on their house. All for playin' loud music and disturbin' the peace. Fire started and the cops and firemen let it burn until the entire square block was nuthin' but ashes. Gone. I saw the whole thing on TV and never forgot. Cops and firemen just standin' around like they at a picnic. Probably thinkin' black folks had no business with those kind a homes in the first place."

She filled both glasses and settled down.

"Didn't mean to go off on a Lenox Avenue soapbox. Ah, you too young to remember that too. Probably just a baby back then."

I nodded. Of course I remembered standing on the corner of 125th and Lenox. It was Lenox Avenue then, and I recall listening to the orators: Black nationalists, Garveyites, Pan-Africans, all preaching pride, self-determination, plus independence for Africa. The crowd was so thick at times I could barely move.

"Anyway, Mali, how'd a pretty young woman like you get mixed up with James? If he owe you, you ain't the only one, I can tell you that. Just take a number and step to the back of the line."

"Well," I said, "it's a bit more complicated than that. He was married to a friend of mine and he abused her very badly. She's dead now and—"

"Whoa. What a minute." Miss Dottie put her glass down and leaned forward, frowning. "Did he do it? You sayin' he killed her?"

"I don't know. The cops don't think so, that's why he's still out here, but . . . I have other ideas. He recently threatened me and I'm trying to find him, to talk to him."

"Well, you outta luck 'cause he on the lam. Skipped out owin' me eight weeks' back rent."

"When did he move?"

"About a week ago. I didn't even know till I checked his room. You see, I have the parlor and street floors. Upstairs, I have three rooms rented. All working folks. Single, quiet, and respectable. But that James . . ." She shook her head and took a sip from her glass. "I guess I was stupid. He talked me into feeling sorry for him and I let him have the room I was gonna rent to my cousin.

"Anyway, for a few days I hadn't heard any footsteps over my head or any of his loud talk, so I said lemme check and see what's happenin'. Maybe he croaked in there or somethin'. But I opened his door and saw he had eased on down the road.

"I sure hope you find him before I do 'cause I'm gonna strip it outta his skin. Use up my gas, my light and electricity, and walked leavin' a room full a funky clothes. What I'm supposed to do with them rags? Boy slicker than goose grease but he gonna get paid. And you know, he also ran up a monster tab—loans and numbers—and Maxie and his crew don't play. They take your legs."

She finished her soda and offered me another glass, which I declined, but I listened for another five minutes. No, she knew none of his relatives, otherwise she would've been kicking their door in. She knew none of his friends but bet they were probably out scouting for him also.

James seemed to have skipped owing half of Harlem. He wasn't likely to roll up on me anytime soon, so I left my personal card and took her phone number.

"You know I'm in the club every Friday," she said. "I love your father's music. Brings back memories, times when there was serious jazz all over Harlem."

"It's coming back," I said. "Things come full circle if you hang in there long enough."

I said good-bye and headed toward Powell Boulevard, passing the Heaven's Gate Funeral Home and the Sunset Funeral Services.

A minute later I doubled back to Lenox Avenue remembering that Alvin wanted Häagen-Dazs butter pecan and I wanted mango-raspberry sorbet. The flyer from the supermarket near 130th Street advertised it and the price was right.

chapter

thirteen

"So what you sayin'? I gotta pay you seventy a week now? An extra twenty?"

"That's right. I need to pay for this TV."

Ache stood in the doorway of the junk-filled living room and stared at Hazel and then at the television, a thirty-three-inch behemoth propped on the pyramid of milk crates where the old twelve-inch set once rested. The old one, smashed, had been taken out by the two men who'd sold her the new model. They'd scooped it, they said, as "it fell off the back of a truck'' and figured she'd be interested, seein' as how she was disabled and not able to get around and all . . .

"And 'cause your boy's our boy, we lettin' it go for just a couple dollars down and then twenty dollars a week," they had said.

Once they'd hooked it up, Hazel had not bothered to ask how many weeks. She had given them what was left of her SSI check and then sat there as if she'd been planted, mesmerized by Jerry Springer, Ricki Lake, and Jenny Jones.

No, she didn't like Oprah. Didn't go for her at all. The nerve of that black woman earning a million a minute. The nerve of her losing all that weight. And had that fine, fine man draped on her arm. No, she didn't like Oprah at all, at all.

She felt so much better watching those young girls, hair flying, duking it out over some grinning man on Jerry's show. Or watching the fat woman crying on "Jenny Jones" when the ex-husband, same size, confessed he couldn't cut it anymore and Jenny, her face pinched with as much concern as plastic would allow, offering last-minute counseling as the credits rolled.

"I got to pay 'em twenty every Friday," Hazel said, briefly pulling her eyes away from the screen to count the money he'd handed her. "Listen," she continued. Her voice remained in the low normal octaves because she did not want to miss a line of Jerry Springer running up the steps to push the mike under someone's outraged nose. "It's more'n you thought a doin' for me. TV in pieces on the floor and you didn't give a shit. If it wasn't for Junebug next door, tellin' me how this set was available, I don't know where I'd be."

Jerry broke for a commercial and allowed Hazel to devote her full attention to her son. "And shit, seventy dollars a week is cheap. Where you gonna pay that for a place to lay your stupid head. Remember couple years ago you thought you could do better and walked out with your ass on your shoulder. Bronx ate you up, didn't it? Lucky your room was here when you come crawlin' back . . ."

He leaned against the wall, remembering and feeling the rage well up in him again.

Fat sloppy bitch. Ass on my shoulder? You come in on me in the bathroom, bust in like you the Five-O with a fuckin' no-knock warrant. Me, I'm standin' there. You starin' and laughin'.

Memory came back and hit him in the face. Hazel standing with her arms in a tight knot across her chest like a judge passing sentence, and her voice—loud and hoarse from laughing.

". . . coulda told you all along you was wastin' your money. All them pills 'n' shit. Ain't done nuthin'. Dick still small as the day you was born. Steroids ain't done shit 'cept shrink your wallet. That's money coulda been comin' my way. You ain't got nuthin' hangin'. Just like your no-good daddy . . ."

He'd left in the middle of the night, ran to the Bronx, and got an equally dirty room and a job bagging and stocking groceries in a small supermarket. The few months he was there—

three women, ordinary to the point of anonymity while living, but spectacular in death—restored his balance, and Hazel's laughter eventually faded. He'd kept the news clippings
but was furious at the lack of detail. No mention of the cereal.
Didn't they know the cereal was important? The dumb cops
weren't doing their job.

Now he looked at Hazel sprawled on the couch, her dress
hiked between her knees. The same dress she'd put on day
after day after day until some parts had stiffened from the dirt
and grease. He peered at the table in front of her piled high
with empty food containers where the residue had hardened
to a black crust.

The commercial died and she pulled a family-size box of
frosted cornflakes onto her lap, dug in, and put a fist to her
mouth, chewing absently. Like popcorn at the movies.

He stared at the box and a wave of revulsion rose in his
throat, knotting his tongue so that he couldn't speak.

The crunching noise followed as he retreated down the
hall to his room, where he closed the door to shut out the
sound. He sat on the edge of the bed and gazed into the blank
darkness.

Cereal. Stuffin' her face with it. That same cereal . . .

Even in the dark, his head started to spin and he tried to
shift, to think of something else that might ease the pressure.

*Twenty dollars more a week. I ain't even watchin' no TV.
Twenty dollars. Only time I looked was when they had my man,
Jeffrey Dahmer, on. Hell, I had to see him. He was famous. Now*

I gotta give up twenty more? How long she got to pay? Bet the fuck she don't even know.

He leaned forward and unfolded the small paper bag he'd brought home. It contained one of the borderline-fresh rolls the store gave away to the help at the end of each day. An alternative to having them remain in the bin overnight as entrees for various nocturnal crawlers.

He broke the roll open with his thumbs and stuffed it with the slices from the ham and the cheese packets he'd stolen during the day. That and a warm can of the cheapest soda he'd made a big show of paying for when he checked out. He ate in the murky glow of the fifteen-watt light near his bed, licking his fingers, then wiping them against the edge of the worn blanket.

He had eaten like this for days, weeks, months. Couldn't remember when last he'd been in the kitchen to warm up a pot of soup or plug in a coffeepot. The last time, before he'd run up to the Bronx, he'd stepped in the kitchen in the middle of the night for a glass of water and witnessed a mass movement over the crusted dishes piled in the sink.

He had switched off the lights and sneaked back to his room, past his mother snoring on the couch in front of the blank television, and stuffed the cracks under his door with rags. But in the morning, every morning, he watched vermin scatter under the stained tile in the bathroom when he switched on the light. He watched them fall thick and fast as he shook out his towel and sour facecloth at arm's length. He held his toothbrush under boiling water, and when the water wasn't hot, he didn't bother to brush at all. No point in picking up more germs.

And he'd settled for the dinners patched together with stolen cold cuts. When he felt flush, he sat at the counter in Pan Pan's in the last seat, breathing in the steam from a bowl of soup.

Hazel never noticed that she hadn't cooked for her son in twenty years. She ordered out and alternated between pizza and Chinese and, when she was flush, barbecue dinners.

Occasionally one of her "overnighters"— all of whom she called "Pop" because they popped in and right back out, rarely staying more than twenty-four hours—brought a bucket of fried chicken.

When Ache had returned from the Bronx, it seemed that the same dishes were still in the sink and the same smelly cartons were still on the floor.

Now he placed the sandwich wrapping and empty can in a plastic bag and tied it in a tight knot. He thought of turning on a brighter light but the unshaded fifteen-watt ceiling bulb was too much for him. The light penetrated his head sometimes and made it hurt like all those lights in the store.

People starin' like they had nuthin' better to do.

But he needed the job. Where could he go?

But I got to go somewhere. Somewhere else. Bitch come in the place tonight, just as we closin'. Funny eyes. Look right at me like she know somethin'. All the while, sweet-talkin' that stupid-ass manager she want ice cream. He had the lock on the door and opened back up just for her. Fuckin' ice cream can't nobody even pronounce the name of. And him grinnin' from ear to ear watchin' them long legs, watchin' that ass move down the aisle like she got a engine in it.

He squirmed on the bed, remembering how she had turned around, approaching him at the checkout, and the tight shrinking he'd felt when she'd gazed at him. At first, a shock had passed through him. He was staring at the eyes of Mercy Anne. He was back in the sixth grade once more, sitting directly behind her. Only now these eyes were different. They were stronger, bolder, unafraid.

And goddamn laughin' like she saw somethin' funny.

He had felt the panic tighten his chest, cutting his breath, but at the same time, he fought to keep the elation under control. Mercy Anne. He never thought he'd get a second chance.

He watched her leave the store and he'd left the manager alone to struggle with the lock. Shit, that was his job anyway.

And he trailed the funny eyes, keeping to the shadows, several feet behind her. Strivers' Row. Waited in the thick shadow of the trees across the street. Waited almost two hours.

And the bitch come back out trottin' a fuckin' horse. But I'm a do somethin'. Show her who to laugh at.

He removed his shirt and pants and hung them on the nail behind the door, then sat on the bed again, his hands fingering the sagging edges of the mattress, waiting.

Finally, when the voice, a whisper in the dark, came to him, the message confused him at first.

Looka here, Ache. This time, you could get two for one. A two for one. You ain't never did that before. This'll put you over.

The voice faded, leaving him alone in the silence. Then he smiled and snapped his fingers at the brilliance of the idea. *Two for one. How 'bout that. Both of 'em got to go. Funny Eyes and that other one. Look right through me like I wasn't there.*

He moved to lie down near the light and to read again the scrap of the article he'd torn out of the *Amsterdam News* two days earlier.

Felicia Temple, well-known Harlem artist, will exhibit her paintings at the Studio Museum Sunday afternoon 1–6 p.m.

The museum. That ain't nuthin'. I already been to her house. Couple times.

But he had only seen her one time. It was the housekeeper or someone else who usually did the shopping who'd come to the door. Ms. Temple was too busy. The first time, he hadn't known any better and went up the steps to the front door. When the lady who was probably the housekeeper opened it, he had caught a momentary glimpse of an eighty-foot expanse of polished hardwood floor flowing from foyer to living room to dining room filled with pictures and a style and abundance of furniture he'd never seen before.

The crystal chandeliers blinded him but that was not important. He could always escape from those kinds of light.

The wood carvings were another matter. They were huge masks decorated with beads and shells and some kind of tangled straw. And empty space where sight should have been. But he imagined them angled down from the walls, looking at him.

"You must be new," the lady who was probably the housekeeper said as she pointed over the brass railing. "The groceries are usually delivered through the downstairs entrance."

She had smiled and said "son," so the fear and anger that had ballooned in his chest dissolved to a dull ache. Now he felt nothing, no anger toward the housekeeper, a short, round woman who kept pushing her glasses back on her dark face and who could have been his grandmother—if he knew who his grandmother was. But he didn't know. Didn't know his grandfather either. Or his father for that matter.

He could not reach back in memory because there was nothing there, only a midnight that frightened him whenever he thought about it. So he remained in the present with his mother and her wall of rage. It was all he knew.

The lady had pointed and he had taken the box through the wrought-iron door under the steps, through the long, carpeted hall with the gleaming wainscoting, lugging the box to the kitchen at the back of the house where everything including the hanging pots and pans glowed silver.

"Remember to always bring it through this way," the lady said as she reached into a vase on the pantry shelf for his tip.

He had waited impatiently, eyes roving, and saw the garden and the easel and the tall, thin lady who stepped away from the easel with her hand to her chin, like she was studying something only she could see.

He had stared at her brown skin and silver-white hair pulled back in a smooth ball. He could not guess how old she was, only that she was so beautiful he'd stopped breathing for a moment. Her jeans and T-shirt were paint-spattered but in the enclosure of greenery she looked like somebody in the movies.

Not . . . not like them skanks all spread out in those magazines.

"Here you are," the housekeeper said.

He reached for the two dollars, not knowing what to say, so he said nothing.

Outside, he looked up and down 136th Street for someplace to sit, to ease the tight feeling in his chest, but there were no benches, so he walked across St. Nicholas Avenue and sat near the park.

Faces with no eyes.

He leaned over on the bench and felt the sweat run down the back of his neck and down his chest, causing the shirt to stick to his skin. He waited for the familiar voice to come and tell him what he should do but there was only silence.

He opened his eyes as a group of day campers wearing red and black T-shirts and black shorts passed by, escorted by three teenage counselors, one in the front, middle, and rear. The day campers held hands, laughed, and shouted nursery rhymes to a rap beat.

The sun bore down and his shirt felt clammy. He stared at the small faces through half-closed eyes, looking for the ugly one and wondering what the child was feeling. But all the faces were smiling, so it was hard to tell who the ugly one was. And who had been shut in darkness with nothing but a box of cereal.

He watched until they turned and disappeared into the park at 140th Street. His breathing was not so ragged now and his chest didn't hurt as much, so he left the bench and made his way back to the store.

That had been two days ago. Now he lay on the bed in the dim glow thinking of the women. Mercy Anne and her dead white eyes had come back on those long legs to laugh all over again. And that woman in the garden, all that dead white hair rolled in a ball against her neck. And those stupid masks. She put them up there, to look down on him.

He folded the scrap of paper carefully and tucked it in the space between the sagging mattress and box spring where he kept the other news clippings and the pages and ads from *Soldier of Fortune*, *Body Builder*, and *Hustler*.

Studio Museum. Okay.

Loud laughter drifted down the hall and he heard Hazel stomp her feet a few times but he eventually managed to fall asleep. In his dreams, he had gotten two for one. The headlines blared. He was on television. He wasn't Jeffrey Dahmer, but Geraldo was shaking his hand anyway, and he was famous.

And he did not wake when the dream morphed into

something else. He was in school again, this time in the principal's office, struggling to remain upright on a steeply angled treadmill. Someone turned the motor and it began to revolve faster and faster but his hands were tied to the railings and he could not free himself. Just ahead, a piece of paper dangled from somewhere just beyond his sight line. Then the print grew like the letters on an optician's chart, small at the bottom, but large enough at the top and growing larger with each revolution of the treadmill to tell him how the free lunch pass that had guaranteed at least one meal a day had been taken away because his mother wouldn't fill out the forms. She wouldn't fill out the forms.

The chart dissolved and he was out of school, standing at a checkout counter, bagging groceries, and at the end of the day all the nickels and dimes he had earned had somehow slipped through his fingers.

chapter

fourteen

The shadow of the Harlem State Office Building loomed large across Adam Clayton Powell Boulevard and cast a shade over the blockfront where the old RKO Alhambra movie theater once stood. The modernized facades, between 125th and 126th Streets, now housed the New York State Motor Vehicle Bureau, a billiard parlor, and a Masonic lodge.

On Sunday the bureau was closed and its doorway provided a niche for a Senegalese vendor to sell sunglasses. When

Ache approached, the peddler dipped into his canvas bag and came out with nine different styles dangling from his fingers.

Ache chose the glasses with the darkest lenses and tried them on under the glow of the vendor's brilliant smile. "It look good, brother. Look good."

He said nothing but folded the glasses and slipped the vendor a ten-dollar bill. The vendor temporarily closed shop, keeping his eyes peeled for another customer or a roving "quality of life" patrol car, whichever came first.

He donned the glasses, made his way across the avenue, and sat on one of the stone benches dotting the plaza and scrutinized the crowd. Several minutes later he moved slowly across 125th Street and, hidden behind the lenses, entered the museum.

In the corridor he stared in surprise at the smiling young woman behind the admission desk.

Five dollars. I got to pay five dollars to walk in here. Shit. Bust a hole in my pocket. Ten for the glasses and now five to get in. Shit.

He felt the bile churn up in his throat and wondered whether he should swallow or bathe the smile off the girl's face with the hot splash of his saliva. But a uniformed guard was standing at attention less than three feet away. And besides, he really did want to see the lady with the silver hair.

So he parted with the money and moved along the narrow corridor. He peeped in the store that sold books and beautiful souvenirs but the lights, too bright, kept him out. He could not remember a time when he'd liked bright lights. Perhaps when he had been very young; before his mother discovered the power of the locked closet.

The first time, he had screamed, banged his head against the door until stars danced before him. The second time, he had cried again but did not bang his head so hard. The times after that, he gradually accepted the darkness as a natural part of his world. He did not close his eyes, did not fold into the familiar knot, but stretched out on the fetid rags layering the floor.

When the voices began, they confused him at first because there had been so many. The one he liked best was the one who called him "Ache," told him how smart he was to take darkness as a hideout.

You cool, Ache. Slick. Long as you can think in the dark, what you need light for? Can't run up on nobody at high noon. Think about that . . .

The voice that called him "Ache" silenced the others, inverted his fear of dark to light so that when he was thrown in the closet again, his only concern was that he would be ignored, overlooked, forgotten, and perhaps left to starve to death. The memory of the dark steadied him as he edged cautiously along the hall and entered the main gallery.

He had never been inside a place like this—a large, two-tiered room where people moved in a slow parade, brochures in hand, pausing to study each picture. Lights shone directly on the paintings, so he did not look at them.

Somewhere in the crowd, a woman's voice filtered up, explaining that the Studio Museum had originally opened in

1967 in a rented loft on upper Fifth Avenue to showcase the works of black artists who were excluded from gallery and museum shows downtown. At that time, only Jacob Lawrence, Elizabeth Catlett, and Romare Beardon had general national exposure.

The museum opened at its current site in 1982, and visiting artists were regularly sent to Harlem's schools to help children develop an appreciation for the fine arts.

The woman spoke to the crowd and he eased forward, then stopped. The voice did not belong to Felicia Temple. This woman was too short, her hair was dark, and she wore glasses, so he stopped listening and wandered away.

He stepped into the garden where a loose knot of a dozen or so people were standing in the sun examining the sculpture and murmuring among themselves. A faint breeze ruffled the wide brim of a woman who stood apart from the group. When she turned, he saw that she was not the one.

He moved back inside, and the tight squeezing he thought had gone away now returned. It spread beyond his throat and dropped anchor in his chest. Felicia Temple wasn't here. Maybe she didn't even exist. He thought of the masks again and confusion overwhelmed him. Maybe it had been the ghost of one of those others, standing at that easel in the garden. Maybe no one had been there at all.

He headed for the steps leading to the second floor and took them two at a time, nearly knocking over the waiter walking down with a platter balanced above his head.

"Whyn't the fuck you look where you goin'?"

The waiter stared in surprise, then stepped around him gingerly, as if circumventing a large rodent. A man and a woman standing directly behind the waiter stared at Ache, then looked away, shaking their heads.

By the time he reached the top of the stairs, his stomach had churned into a loop of pain and it was hard to concentrate. He saw a line forming near a large reception table decorated with trays of food. There was a line near the bar also.

He listened to the chink of plates and utensils and gazed at the food and wondered how much it cost. Was it free? No one was reaching into their pockets. It was free. So were the drinks. He watched the women on the line reach into the trays for small things to place on their plates.

She was not there. Nor was she at the bar where long thin glasses were filled and refilled with a sparkling wine. He turned to retreat down the stairs when the three-piece combo—flute, bass, and drums—struck up, sending a soft fanfare of sound over the room. He glanced to the right of the musicians and saw her sitting at a small glass table with two men and another woman. Sweat made his palms slippery as he adjusted his glasses. He had nearly missed her.

She was laughing at something but the sound did not reach him. She leaned forward to shake someone's hand, and the sleeve of the red loose-knit silk sweater slanted off her shoulder. Her hair glimmered in the indirect lighting.

Behind his sunglasses, he could make out the movement of her mouth and he wanted the words to spill over him. He wanted her to raise her hand and wave and smile; her eyes to follow him and let everyone know that she knew him. And they would all smile and nod approvingly.

But she raised a shawl of some kind to her shoulders and the two men and the woman rose when she did. A second later the glass table was empty.

Two days later, as he packed groceries, he listened to the lady who was the housekeeper chatting with the cashier.

"I know this is a large delivery, but I'm going out of town for a few days. My niece's getting married in Florida and I'm going down to help her mama. Make sure that woman put the right fork in the right place on the right table, you know what I mean? Some folks want to do things right but just don't know how. I'm leaving next Tuesday."

He listened as the cashier said, "I know what you mean. There's so much to think about when it comes to weddings. Especially big ones. A thousand things can go wrong just like that."

He bowed his head. He did not want the woman to recognize or remember him.

chapter

fifteen

I did not get to Dr. De's until Saturday morning, a week later. And only after Dad had looked at me closely, then asked if I needed "walking around" money. And after Alvin, more directly, did a pretty good imitation of Eddie Murphy baying at the moon when I had come down to breakfast.

I'd had no time for hair grooming. I was still at war with myself trying to adjust to the idea that James might not have killed Marie and that he might not have been responsible for Claudine either.

When I stepped into the crowded barbershop, Dr. De, Smitty, and Charlie each had at least four people waiting. ". . . and that's not counting the folks who took a number and stepped out to the laundermat or the supermarket," a young man said as he moved over on the bench, allowing me to squeeze in.

Dr. De caught my eye and smiled. "Hey, hey, Mali. Good to see you. You number five, okay?" He nodded and clicked his scissors, using his usual psychology. Once a person stepped in, he or she was drawn into the set and leaving was unthinkable. Those who took a number and left, somehow made it back just as the chair was vacated for them.

I removed my scarf, and my reflection in the mirror stared back, telling me not to bother taking a number, just take a seat and make myself comfortable.

I settled in, glancing at the other faces, and, as usual, felt the familiar warmth and comfort close around like a cocoon. I watched the men, at ease with themselves. When they glanced out the window, the plate glass seemed to provide an additional buffer as they watched the passing parade.

"Hey, that's Kenneth."

"Is that Kenneth? Naw."

"Yes it is." The observer turned from the window and raised his voice like an auctioneer: "Anybody in here kin to Kenny? Know Kenny? Owe Kenny? No? Okay, now we can talk about Kenny."

"Damn. Mack Daddy ain't lookin' too cool," Charlie's customer said. "Done lost the glide in his stride."

"Just got out. How you expect he be walkin' after all them years?"

"Had it goin' on back in the day. Diamond on every finger, and two on his thumbs. Then his dippin' 'n' dabbin' had him grippin' 'n' grabbin'. He be lucky now to even see food stamps."

"Ain't nuthin' sorrier than a broke-ass pimp," Charlie concluded.

In here, where private language prevailed, the verb "to be" was conjugated without igniting a sociological firestorm:

"Yeah, brother. I be gone a few weeks."

"Is that right? Well, I be lookin' after your lady."

"Mm-hmm. And when I git back, you be Dee E Dee. Dead."

In here, slow days were never slow. It only meant that Dr. De could step out to the Sugar Shack and maybe sit down to a meal and rest his feet for forty-five minutes instead of sending for a quick takeout from Pan Pan's.

Slow days meant space enough for the two old historians, eighty-four and ninety-one, to bend knee-to-knee over a chessboard older than they were and work strategy like Hannibal.

Dad got his hair cut on the slow days and sometimes stayed all day.

I preferred Saturdays, when I could catch the latest talk. The television positioned on top of the soda dispenser was turned off and the observers, tired of their window watch, turned to the rap inside.

"So like I was askin' y'all," said Charlie, the middle barber. "Who's really bein' empowered by all this empowerment money?" He raised his scissors and spun the chair in a half-circle to close in on the nape of a young boy, the scissors working the outline of a Coptic cross in low relief against his fade.

"I say it's like this," Charlie continued. "The folks inside the barricade—which is us—ain't gonna see one damn dime a that dollar."

"Tell it, brother," Dr. De nodded. "It's gonna be just like that last War on Poverty. Buccaneers, brokers, and B.S. artists cleaned up while homeboy on the corner singin' 'a change gonna come someday.'

"Soon as you bust one gate, a wall goes up someplace else. The fight goes on."

I glanced at the faces in the silence. Behind the bravado and good humor, everyone in the shop was seeking not just a haircut but respite from shared pain. And, if not a common understanding of why life was the way it was, at least a common idea about how to prevent it from getting any worse.

"You got to see the big picture," Dr. De said. "Those buccaneers, brokers, and B.S. artists, their only contact with the barricades happen when they rattlin' through on Metro-North and gaze out on the scene: Tore-up streets and tenements. Hi-rise cages somebody nicknamed the projects. A 'project' is somethin' you workin' on, experimentin' with, you know what I'm sayin'?

"Some a them dig the scene and don't see a thing. But

there's one—maybe the buccaneer or the bullshitter—pardon me, ladies—shoots a glance and a lightbulb goes on. Bam! Before he hits the Bronx, that dude has figured out how more gold could be scooped from this zone than from a South African mine.''

"Now, wait a minute, brother," a young man said. He was sitting on the bench near the man next to me. "You got it wrong. Sure, back in the day there was a lot of stealin' and dealin'. But what's happenin' now is different."

"How so?"

"Well, the folks are a lot more hip. They're not gonna stand still for no shady stuff. People gettin' busted for the smallest things nowadays."

"You right. It's the small things. Them squeegee guys and jaywalkers know the deal. Crime don't play. P-L-A-Y."

"Ah, you talkin' apples and oranges now."

"Naw we ain't. Crime is crime is crime."

"Except the big boys get community time. Cops get overtime. And we get hard time."

"What you say, brother!"

"Tell it so we know it. That's why we got to stand up for what's real instead of fallin' for whatever they throw our way."

I closed my eyes, leaned back, and rested my head against the wall intending to listen, but I must have fallen asleep. I saw my Grandaunt Celia and heard my mother saying, "Stand up for what's right. Don't let anyone beat you down. Always remember Aunt Celia and how she stood up—"

". . . Mali?"

I had been dreaming. I heard my name. I heard something else but it was outside the dream. I woke and Dr. De was tapping my shoulder.

"You ready or you want to nod? I know some of the B.S. is boring but you really let us know it. You was cuttin' zzzs like a cop on overtime."

I raised my head from the shoulder of a man seated next to me, a complete stranger. I hoped I hadn't drooled on him.

He held up his hand, cutting into my apology. "Don't be sorry. Hey, I'm blessed. Can't remember when somebody pretty as you been within wavin' distance. You still sleepy? Be my guest."

I settled into Dr. De's chair and listened to the talk, trying to piece together what I thought I'd heard: Jobs lost. Numbers missed. Hard times. Food stamps. Food. I wasn't dreaming.

". . . man, you kiddin'," said an older man now seated in Charlie's chair.

"Naw, it was Billy told me. He was shootin' a video over by that supermarket, testin' his camera before a weddin'. Aimed at the window and caught this dude scoopin' a box of cereal. Cornflakes. Right outta somebody's groceries. Caught the brother's hard times right on tape. Said he felt like goin' in there and droppin' coins on 'im but the weddin' party showed up and he let it go."

"Well, they cut welfare everywhere but on Wall Street," Charlie said. "City ate four hundred million in taxes to keep the big boys from jumpin' across the Hudson. But they cut food stamps. Got young girls on the streets pushin' brooms bigger than they are when they should be in school. Got that Gestapo sommabitch downtown talkin' how he gonna cut children off food stamps if the mamas don't take any kinda job come their way."

"Fuckin' power gone to his head."

"And they warehousin' more brothers than they got room for. This just the beginnin'. Folks be snatchin' more than cereal."

I listened through the buzz of the clippers, then shifted suddenly as if a current had passed through the chair.

Dr. De grabbed my neck and held it steady. "Girl, you tryin' to ruin my rep. I almost cut a groove in your scalp. Hold on a minute and you can go home and slide into a coma if you want."

I held up and, twenty minutes later, walked out with a business card I picked from the flyers and ads posted near the door.

Outside on the crowded avenue, I ignored the sun beating time like a drummer on my newly exposed scalp. I concentrated instead on the elaborately fancy print on the card in my hand.

Memories Fade
But Weddings Christenings and Parties
Live Forever on Film
Call Video Billy for Appointment

chapter

sixteen

After an awkward pause, Tad seemed elated to hear from me and gladder about the latest news.

"A box of cereal, Mali? On video?"

"That's what I understand . . ."

"Listen, I'm coming over. Okay?"

And ten minutes later he knocked at the door.

When I opened it and gazed at his deepset eyes, his honeyed skin, and the silver in his close-cut hair, I almost forgot why I'd called him. I focused on his black silk shirt open at the throat and studied the soft pleat in his gray linen trousers until my head cleared somewhat.

He sat on the edge of the sofa and listened, then shook his head. "Maybe something to it. Maybe not."

"What else do we have to go on right now?" I said as I dialed Billy's number. Luckily he was at home.

We walked the few blocks to St. Nicholas Avenue and then south toward 133rd Street, making small talk after I'd related the conversation in Dr. De's, but mostly we walked in silence.

The elevator was old and sluggish and we were alone. I stared at the flickering indicator like a stranger as the floors moved by, much too slow to suit me.

"Nice haircut," he said.

"Thanks," I replied, studying the walls as if they were hung with rare paintings. The silence closed in and I wanted to close my eyes.

"Still mad at me?" he whispered.

He was behind me now and his hands eased around my shoulders to turn me around. "Still mad?"

He pressed me against him and I breathed in his cologne. I could feel the fast hard rhythm in his chest. My arms flew up and around him and I backed him against the wall. It was easy to do because he was willing, and right now I needed him to be willing. His mouth opened and I tasted mint and wanted to swallow his tongue. His mustache tickled and I wondered if the elevator had ever gotten stuck between floors.

"You're not still mad, are you, baby?"

"About what?" I whispered.

His mouth covered my ear now and I heard his breathing and felt the dizzyingly familiar rhythm of the rest of him. When the door slid open with a noisy groan, I was soaked, stressed, and ready to see Billy another time, any other time but now.

It took a few minutes to get myself together, so we lingered in the corridor, glancing around at the mottled beige walls and etched-glass light fixtures. The mauve carpet leading from the elevator was soft and thick.

The apartment was on the fifth floor of a seven-story limestone facing the steep green rise of St. Nicholas Park. It was an old building, kept intact by the strength of the locked lobby door and the will of the older tenants who remembered how it used to be "when you could sleep on your fire escape on a muggy night without getting mugged."

We rang the bell and waited. Footsteps approached behind the door and Billy opened it with a flourish.

"How are you?" he whispered, gazing at Tad as if he were a birthday present sent special delivery from Neiman-Marcus.

"I'm fine," I said, even though he hadn't even seen me. "I'm Mali Anderson and this is Detective Tad Honeywell."

"Yes. You're the one who called," and looking at Tad, he said, "A detective. My, my, my. I'm sure you must do very interesting work. A detective."

Billy was about five-nine, with locked hair down to his

shoulders and eyes that reminded me of old amber. He wore a white top and drawstring pants made of light East Indian cotton.

"The place is a wreck," he said. "Y'all gotta excuse me. This week I've been too busy to clean anything except my body."

He led the way through a narrow foyer with walls covered in red silk and into a living room painted a high-gloss chocolate and every inch covered with artwork: oil on canvas, acrylic on Masonite, mixed media on paper, acrylic and pastel on board, and pen-and-ink studies.

The sun filtered through a collection of old blue glass bottles arranged in tiers in the curtainless windows, and the room was furnished entirely with antiques. I did not see a speck of dust.

"Have a seat," he said, waving us toward a burgundy velvet sofa. "I know you could use something cool to drink. Beer, iced tea, or soda?"

"Soda," Tad said.

He stepped into a small kitchen and this gave me a chance to look closely at the artwork.

When he returned, I was staring at a ten-by-twelve-inch drawing by Keith Haring. It had been inscribed to Billy.

"You knew Keith Haring?"

Billy nodded. His teeth were perfect when he smiled. "Knew him way before he became famous," he said, placing a large bottle of ginger ale on the coffee table. "Played handball together in the East Village years ago. I never had the work appraised because I don't ever intend to sell it."

"I don't blame you," I said.

He opened an old ebony cabinet inlaid with ivory paneling and brought out three cut-crystal glasses. "Now, let's see. Just soda or would y'all like it mixed with something stronger?"

"Soda is fine," I said, settling back on the sofa. "You're quite a collector. Your place is filled with such beautiful things."

He smiled again as he filled the glasses, pleased that I'd noticed. Then he positioned himself on a leather ottoman with his legs curled under him yoga style, ready to talk business.

"You said you wanted to speak to me about a video? What's the occasion?"

"Well, actually," I said, "the occasion has passed."

Billy looked from me to Tad, then back at me, his eyes narrowing. "Passed? You want me to video a funeral? Darling, I don't do funerals. Only fun things. My nerves can't take no grim stuff."

"No," I said. "This was a wedding took place maybe a few weeks ago. You were taping it, but first you had tested your equipment near a church, near a supermarket, and caught someone in the window taking some groceries. Do you recall that?"

Billy placed his glass on the table and leaned forward with his hands under his chin. "Do I remember. Do I remember. It was right outside the Good Tidings African Apostolic Church on Lenox Avenue. Supermarket's right next door.''

I looked at Billy. "Is it a small church with a white front next to that new supermarket near 130th Street?''

"That's the one. We ain't hardly talkin' cathedral here,'' Billy said.

"Do you have the tape?'' Tad said. "We're trying to find the man who took that box of cereal.''

"Boy, I don't believe this,'' Billy sighed, throwing up his hands. "I heard of 'quality of life' offenses, but I can't believe a detective, a detective lieutenant no less, is assigned to look for a cereal thief. That fool in City Hall must not have anything else to think about.''

"This guy is wanted for something else,'' I said.

Billy looked at me again, then narrowed his eyes even further. "Oh! What?''

"Right now we can't say because he may very well be innocent. But once we see the tape, we'll be able to—''

"Well, that's just it. I don't have it.''

"Not even a copy?'' Tad asked, a look coming over his face that said he didn't believe him.

"Not even a copy. And that's not like me to bypass something like that. But—well, here's what happened. The bride was so anxious to see the tape, I gave it to her with the understanding that it hadn't been edited or anything. There was a lot of stuff, raw stuff, that I planned to cut out. For one thing, her man's mama had drunk too much and fell off her chair and I needed to take that out. Plus there was a fistfight near the punch bowl and some girl got separated from her weave. I'm tellin' you, some colored folks just need to stay home till they can get their act together.

"So a week goes by and she doesn't return the tape, doesn't call, or anything. I mean I practically jammed her machine with at least a hundred messages and not one call was returned. Well, lo and behold, when I finally caught up with her—must have called on an off day—she said she had no intention of giving me back the tape. She said she'd destroyed it."

"Why would she do that?" I asked, aware now that Tad probably wanted me to do most of the talking. Billy was making the most of his bold amber eyes and Tad, behind his bland professionalism, was not at ease.

Billy lifted his shoulders in a slow, elegant dancer's move. "She claimed I had deliberately angled the camera in such a way as to make her look fat. Please! I'm an artist. Half the paintings on these walls, I did them. I'm a professional. I know my job and this three-hundred-fifty-pound heifer with a behind so wide you could sit on didn't need no help from me or my camera. She was fat before video was invented. Period.

"I don't believe she destroyed that tape and I got her broad behind in court right now to get my money. A deal is a deal. And if you ask me, she shoulda invested in a little Slim-Fast before she cornered the market on spandex."

I took a sip of my soda, waiting for the two snaps up, but he calmed down and continued. "But yes, the supermarket was right next to that two-by-four church she got hitched in. All I saw in the window was the hands and arms, dark, and with enough muscle to lift a car. Why was that man—and it had to be a man—into small shit like pilferin' groceries? I know times are hard, what with these cutbacks and all, but with arms like that, he could be pullin' big dollars in professional wrestling.''

''Could we have the name and address of the bride?'' I asked.

''With pleasure,'' Billy said, moving quickly from the ottoman to get his appointment book. He thumbed through the pages, and when he looked up, his amber eyes shone. ''Here it is. Now, let's see the heifer get attitude with you.''

chapter

seventeen

We were quiet in the elevator until Tad said, "You asked about the supermarket?"

We stepped out into the lobby and hit the sidewalk. I wondered if the tape had been destroyed or if the bride, embarrassed, was simply holding on to it. I wondered about the strong hands lifting the cereal. Were there any tattoos, marks, or moles visible? Did the guy work at the grocery store? Or was he someone off the street who wandered in to bag groceries?

"I was there a few nights ago. For ice cream."

"What happened?"

"Nothing particularly. Place had already closed but the manager let me in. Only one other person was in there. A man, but I barely glimpsed him. I was mainly thinking about Häagen-Dazs butter pecan."

He nodded and glanced at his watch. "Want to take a walk uptown?"

"To see the bride?"

"I was thinking about it . . ."

"I also thought you wanted to work a solo thing."

He looked away, drew a breath of deep exasperation, then gazed at me again. "Mali. Don't make this hard on me. I said I was sorry, didn't I?"

"So you did. Kinda . . ."

I glanced down St. Nicholas Avenue while trying to make up my mind, trying to decide if the tension that had risen between us the last time was because of my attitude toward James or the fact that I was intruding into an area best left to the police. After all, Tad was the detective, and I was only—it took me a while to say it—only an ordinary person relying mainly on intuition and street smarts to get to the bottom of things.

An ordinary person with an ounce of common sense would know to leave well enough alone and let the police do whatever they're supposed to do. Stay out of the way.

But to hell with it. Common sense was in short supply tonight, and when I gazed up into Tad's deep, gold-flecked eyes, logic left also.

"Aah, what're we doing afterward?"

"What would you like?" he whispered. His fingers touched the side of my face, describing a slow arc around my left eyebrow, ear, and under my chin. "Whatever you want, baby, you know I'm for it."

All I could do was smile as I grabbed his hand and moved away from the lobby door for the short walk uptown.

The bride's name was Isabelle Oliver and lived with her husband, Duncan, on Bradhurst Avenue near 148th Street in a small three-room apartment facing Jackie Robinson Park.

When she opened the door, we saw that Billy had not exaggerated. She was five feet four and weighed somewhere in the neighborhood of three hundred pounds. Her face was dark and round and extremely pretty with large eyes and a mouth that seemed ready to let out a sigh, and when she smiled, she showed bright, beautiful teeth. She had a child's face, and despite her size, it was evident that she was very young, maybe twenty, twenty-two at most.

She looked at Tad's shield and her eyes grew larger. "Oh, what happened? Somethin' happened? Oh, God. Somethin' bad happened. I know it!"

Her voice rose, bringing her husband from out of the bedroom. "Muffin! What's goin' on? What's the matter?"

"Oh, Daddy. It's the police. Somethin' happened."

"Nothing's happened," I said, trying to calm her. "We simply need to speak to you about a video that was taken at your wedding. We need to—"

At the mention of the video, Muffin's hands flew to her chest. "I knew it, Daddy. That Billy has put the police on us. That dog!"

She looked as if she was about to collapse and I stood near the door in mild anxiety wondering who was going to help Daddy catch her. But she managed to lean on his arm and make her way into the living room, where she settled into a black leather La-Z-Boy recliner.

We stepped inside, following them. The living room was simply furnished with a green chenille-covered sofa, a small glass coffee table, and a dining table and two chairs which the kitchen was too small to accommodate. An old iron plant stand with a pot trailing bright green ivy down to the floor stood near the window, catching the fast-fading light. A small television was on a shelf over the dining table, and the recliner, with its new-leather fragrance, dominated everything. The place was crowded but clean.

Daddy, who introduced himself as Duncan Oliver, went into the bathroom and returned with a wet cloth to place over Isabelle's face.

"You take it easy, baby. Daddy's gonna see what's what. You just relax."

We remained standing as he arranged the cloth, then adjusted the chair so that Muffin's head rested back like she was ready for a dental exam. He patted her shoulder and then turned to us.

"Have a seat. I'm sorry, but my wife ain't able to take too much excitement. Blood pressure's too high, is what it is. Plus her mama got heart trouble. So any little thing likely to set her off, you know."

He waited for us to sit on the sofa before he moved a chair from the dining table to sit facing us. Duncan Oliver was about five feet ten, 150 pounds, and appeared to be about fifty years old. He had strong features with a prominent nose and a gray pencil mustache that ended in a curve around the sides of his full mouth.

"We only been married a month, and—"

"Four weeks, three days, and eleven hours," Muffin called from under the cloth draped on her face. "And you lovin' every minute of it, ain't you, Daddy?"

"Aah, baby. We got company now."

He squirmed in the chair, smiling embarrassment but couldn't quite pull it off. His smile could not conceal his enormous pride at having such a young and pretty wife. And he clearly liked women of substance.

"Isabelle my second wife," he said, aware that we were aware of the age difference. "First one died two years ago and I didn't think I could ever be happy again till I met Isabelle."

"One Sunday at church, Daddy."

"Yeah. I heard this voice singin' in the choir and I said to myself I got to meet this lady, I said—"

"Well, that's wonderful, Mr. Oliver. Congratulations,"

Tad said, cutting into the testimonial that Mr. Oliver seemed prepared to deliver into the next hour.

"We're looking for a person who may be on the video that was taken at your wedding."

"Oh," Isabelle groaned, removing the cloth from her face and adjusting the lever so that she sat upright. She was fully recovered and her voice now had enough timbre to give marching orders to a regiment.

"Listen. I knew it was gonna be trouble. That was my cousin from Philly I wasn't even speakin' to. The woman showed up empty-handed—not even a motel ashtray for a present—then opened her pocketbook and pulled out a doggy bag the size of a shoppin' cart.

"I mean Mashika's one triflin' woman and I sure didn't invite her. The minute I saw her so-called boyfriend, I knew stuff was gonna go down. He look like he just got cut loose from upstate and ain't had a meal with meat in it since he been out. He wasn't dippin' in the food, he was divin' in nose-first, stuffin' his face like a pig.

"I don't know where she gets 'em from but I always say if you lay down with dogs, you gonna get up with fleas, and I mean when she wasn't packin' that doggy cart, she was scratchin' mighty hard."

"Now, Muffin, don't go gettin' your pressure up," Duncan whispered when she paused to catch her breath.

"Well, it's true and the truth is the light, ain't it? The boyfriend started conversatin' on a girl near the punch bowl and Mashika didn't go for it. Came over and read the girl—

Edna, I think her name was. Mind you, Mashika ain't said boo to that dog, but gonna read the girl, tellin' her she wasn't all that.

"Well, Mashika and Edna got into it. And Edna tore that worn-out weave outta Mashika's head, ripped it right on out, which showed you what a cheap job it was. Probably one a them Monday Specials. How she could make such a fool of herself—and at my weddin'—is beyond me."

Isabelle fell silent, exhausted from the speech. She rested her head back against the recliner and her breathing was audible from where we sat.

Duncan disappeared into the kitchen and quickly returned with a glass of water and a small bottle of pills.

"Here, baby. Now, you just relax. Relax."

"Well," Tad said as Isabelle was busy with the pills. She was having trouble swallowing and held the pills in her mouth, swishing them around a few seconds before squeezing her eyes shut and making an enormous gulping sound.

"We'd like to take a look at the video, if you still have it," Tad said. "If the person is on there, and if he's caught and convicted, you stand to get a reward."

"What?" Isabelle and Duncan stared at Tad.

"You mean like $10,000 from that TIPS number?" Duncan added.

"You mean he's on America's Most Wanted? I knew it. Looked like a criminal from the jump. What'd I tell you, Daddy? Didn't I say he looked shaky?"

"Well, Muffin, I only had eyes for you that day so it's kinda hard to—"

Tad cleared his throat. "So if it's possible to get a look at the film, we'd be—"

"Why, sure. Why didn't you say so?"

Isabelle rose quickly from the recliner. She was light on her feet and moved fast. She disappeared into the bedroom and we listened as she opened and closed the doors to a closet and slammed a dresser drawer or chest of some sort. Minutes later she emerged, smiling.

"Here it is. We can look at it right here."

"I have to take it with me," Tad said. "We may have to zero in on a face, enlarge it, and photograph it. We have the equipment to do that."

The smile disappeared and she stood in the doorway of the bedroom, trying to decide. She seemed disappointed that her big moment was slipping away. She had wanted to be the one to point out Mashika's no-good man with his dusty jheri-curl and played-out plaid suit.

Finally she said, "You gotta promise me one thing. This ain't goin' back to Billy. Me and him had some words and he got real ugly. Called me outta my name. Now he got me in court. You gotta promise me it ain't gonna end up back in his hands."

"Not a chance. I received it from you. I'll return it to you, okay? You got my word."

She handed the tape to him as if she were releasing a

small child into the care of some unknown custodian. Tad saw her expression and pulled out his card.

"We'll get this back to you in a day or so. If you want to reach me, call this number."

The frown faded into a small smile. "We glad to be of help," she said as we walked to the door.

"Sorry I couldn't offer you anything beside water to drink," Duncan said, "but Muffin's on a special diet and I quit drinkin' and smokin' . . ."

"—since he met me. Ain't that nice?" Isabelle said.

"Now, baby . . ."

It was dark when we stepped out of the house. We turned from Bradhurst Avenue and walked down 148th Street toward Eighth Avenue, passing the spot where the Peacock Bar once stood. Diagonally across, all the buildings fronting the avenue had been demolished to make way for a new police station.

I studied its mammoth size relative to the surrounding structures and recognized the siege mentality built into each brick. I wondered why there were no slots from which the nozzles of heavy assault weapons could slide.

"All they need is a moat and a drawbridge," I said as we walked up the block toward Seventh.

"The moat's in the back," Tad said, "filled with man-eating alligators."

I thought of what my Aunt Celia had gone through at the hands of the police in Charleston and I failed to find the humor in Tad's remark.

We strolled in the middle of the silent street because the buildings on both sides and the old P.S. 90 elementary school were vacant, awaiting renovation, and the sidewalk was a minefield of potholes. At Seventh Avenue we passed Thelma's Lounge and walked downtown.

"You were really cool with the Olivers," I said. "Patience personified."

Tad shrugged. "Could've gotten a warrant but what the hell. Sometimes it pays to go slow and easy. And it worked out. Imagine banging on that door and sticking a search warrant under Muffin's nose. Girl would've collapsed right then and there. And we'd have a nine-eleven, the medics, and possibly a lawsuit. And the media'd have a circus wanting to know what the hell we were looking for in the first place. Sometimes it pays to take it easy."

He said no more and we strolled down Seventh Avenue slowly. His arm came around my shoulder and I felt the tips of his fingers move around my ear like feathers. I glanced up and saw the smile shaping the curve of his mouth.

"Listen," he murmured, "speaking of slow and easy, I was thinking maybe we'd cut over to Wells for some of the chicken and waffles we missed the last time around. Then go back to my place—"

My glands, all of them, had just begun to salivate at the idea when the ring of his phone interrupted. I felt the urge to grab it and grind it into the pavement under my foot, pulverize it and let the dust blow in the wind.

But Tad was listening intently. His face changed and he spoke only to say, "Shit! Be there in a minute."

He snapped it closed, and before I could ask what had happened, he was already moving away from me.

"Something just came in," he said, avoiding my eyes. "I'll call you as soon as I can."

He left me standing on the corner of 145th Street and Seventh Avenue light-headed with frustration. When I'd calmed down enough to find a phone, I dialed Elizabeth. I needed someone to commiserate with, to tell me that better days—and hopefully nights—were coming.

She came on the line sounding so exuberant I was almost embarrassed to tick off my list of petty complaints. Elizabeth had started dating a school administrator, an assistant principal she'd met at an Urban League fund-raiser. I had not yet met him but he was keeping her so busy I had only heard from her twice since Claudine's funeral. Once to tell me that David—that was his name—was six-three and had eyelashes so thick they curled back on themselves, and the second time to leave a message. "The man is interesting. Details to follow." *In-terest-ing* was how she had broken the word up.

Finally, when I'd finished my sad story about Tad leaving me high and dry, she said, "Listen, girl. You gotta have intestinal fortitude—guts—to work a relationship these days. Tad's a special person and you know he loves you. You have to make up your mind to hang in there." Then she added, "What are you going to do now? How about joining us for dinner? We're going over to Wells. I want you to meet David, size him up."

I let out a groan.

"What's the matter?"

"I'm all right. Tad and I were on our way there when he got that call."

"Come without him. When did you ever let something like that stop you?"

I thought about the crispy fried chicken and the peach cobbler with the sugary crust and nearly gave in.

"I don't know, Elizabeth. I don't know. He just left a minute ago and my wound is too fresh to be objective about David. I'll pass. Have fun."

I hung up and walked toward Lenox Avenue, hoping that Pan Pan's had at least one slice of German chocolate cake left. The Better Crust Pie Shop had closed and I needed something to soothe my last frayed nerve.

At Lenox Avenue and 137th Street I passed the crowded seafood stand where batches of porgies and whiting simmered in deep vats of bubbling oil and the vendors shucked clams and oysters for the waiting buyers.

I strolled to the next corner and I suppose if I had concentrated less on the promise of the chocolate cake and more on my surroundings, I might have heard the car approach as I stepped off the curb. I might have understood how it materialized out of the darkness and that its headlights had been suddenly turned off.

"Sister! Sister!"

A warning drowned by the squeal of tires and my sudden scream.

chapter

eighteen

When I woke, I couldn't move. I wanted to call out but my tongue crowded my mouth and I struggled against a mounting wave of panic. I was choking on dust and wondered if this was how people checked out. Choking on dust. Ashes-to-ashes dust. Images raced through my head and collided with a huge shocking riff of pain that cracked through me like a current.

. . . I am not dead. What happened?

Asking myself the question, even without articulating it, caused pain to speed-dial his cousin super-pain. Then I heard a familiar voice, my voice, from far away say, Ooohhh shit . . .

I wanted to close my eyes to shut out the white ceiling but the ceiling was what connected me to life. Behind my closed lids lay a red darkness and a fear of remaining there. Something—a shadow—hovered, blocking the light, and a large stone settled in the center of my chest. The stone had fingers and another wave of pain hit and I heard the oohhh sound again, closer this time. Finally the light and the ceiling came back:

". . . eyes are clearing, pupils back to normal. Miss Anderson? Can you hear me? Blink twice if you can hear me."

. . . Blink twice. Why do I have to blink at all? Why not just say, Of course I can hear you?

But my damn tongue was still stuck to the roof of my mouth. I blinked twice and the voice said if I felt pain I should blink again. I blinked like a broken traffic light, winked until my eyelashes hurt, flicked my lids until something warm flowed through my arm, then spread in my chest, and I floated off on an old and very mellow Joe Simon riff. Cruised away on an ancient plea that resonated down to my toes: "Let me rock you in the cradle of my love." The voice was an echo fading in the wind.

Dad had sung that song to Mom way back when. Why would I remember it now? It was old folks who remembered old things but couldn't remember where they put their keys five minutes earlier.

I still had more than thirty years until I'd be ready for Social Security but I couldn't remember anything. I drifted deeper and another voice, a man's voice, came in, sweet, low, vaguely familiar:

"Baby, you look good enough to eat."

"Leg or breast?"

"What's in between?"

"Dessert. Chocolate, low-fat, and guaranteed to satisfy your sweet tooth."

"Jesus, baby . . ."

The voice sighed and drifted away. Then music, lower, slower, segued into some more old stuff: Aretha, the Dells, the O'Jays. Even Al Green before he met grits and God. I was in a timeless void and could have gone on forever.

I don't know when the fog lifted and the music stopped but the dreams vanished and I heard Dad's voice. "Mali, can you hear me? You had us scared, girl. Really scared. Can you hear me?"

I floated to shore and opened my eyes.

"Scared? Of what? What happened?"

Dad looked like an old man. When Alvin's face came into focus, he also looked old.

"What happened to you guys?" I asked.

They glanced at each other, then at me, but I was staring around. At the hospital curtains, the tall window with its blinds half drawn, the pale pastel color of the bedspread, and finally at the chalk-white plaster of the cast on my left arm and leg and the tubes running into my right arm from a drip line.

"What happened to me?"

"You were hit by a car. You had a concussion, your left arm's broken, your leg's fractured in two places, and your knee is dislocated. You were out of it for a while. They did a scan and there're no blood clots. You were lucky. Someone said you flew about fifteen feet before you hit the ground."

I looked around, trying to recall where I'd been before I'd ended up here. I couldn't remember. Finally I said, "Was anyone else hurt?"

I had visions of a cab jumping a curb and mowing down a line of pedestrians.

"No. Just you. Hit and run. Tad said he'd left you at 145th Street and Seventh. You were hit on 137th and Lenox. Needless to say, he's very upset."

"Yep. And Bertha and Elizabeth too. As a matter of fact, Tad should be along any minute." Dad checked his watch again.

Alvin leaned over my shoulder to kiss my forehead and I felt his tears. "Aunt Mali. You're gonna be okay. You're gonna be—" He straightened up and left the room to stand outside in the hallway. I listened to him blowing his nose.

"Boy was worried, Mali. Plenty worried."

"He must've been. Imagine calling me *Aunt* Mali. Makes me feel like I'm ninety years old."

"Yeah, well. We were all worried."

Dad cleared his throat. I saw that his eyes were also full, and behind the unshed tears was an anxiety I'd never seen before. I wanted to hug him to me and let him know that I was going to be all right and from now on I would be more careful. Look both ways. Cross at the green. I wanted to hug him but the cast was heavier than it looked and my other arm was also immobilized.

"Dad. Go and see about Alvin. Make sure he's all right."

He rose at once, and the activity, the act of having something to do, having to see about someone else's comfort, restored him. I watched until he walked out, then I closed my eyes. A hit-and-run. Was the driver drunk? High? Had he had a dizzy spell? Was he blabbing on a cell phone while trying to maneuver through traffic and lost control?

I was tired suddenly but snapped awake when I felt the soft mustache brush the side of my mouth, then kiss me full on the lips. I tasted the familiar flavor, saw Tad's half-closed eyes and the small dimple in his chin and the silver in the edge of his hair, and nearly broke my other arm in an effort to hold him to me.

"Mali. You had us all goin' for a while, girl. You had us goin'."

"I'm sorry. This is all probably my fault. My own carelessness. I should've watched where I—"

His finger went to my mouth, then he kissed me again. "Don't say anything. Not now. You're gonna be all right and that's what matters. That's what counts. You're gonna be walkin' out of here in a couple more weeks. Then we can talk about it. I love you, baby. I love you.''

Two weeks and more X rays and another CAT scan and I was fitted with a plastic leg brace and released. I left the room in a wheelchair with Dad and Alvin walking beside me. A plain clothes officer who was sitting at the end of the corridor accompanied us onto the elevator, through the lobby, and out to the curb where Tad was waiting with the motor running. He helped maneuver me into the front seat, gave Tad a thumbs-up, then walked across Lenox Avenue and disappeared into the noonday crowd.

I watched as Tad buckled me into the front seat. My left side felt stiff and a flash of pain shot through me as I tried to turn around.

''That officer, he a friend of yours?'' I asked, trying to ignore my discomfort.

''You might say that.''

Dad and Alvin were silent and I could feel something building as we cruised along. Finally I said, ''Was the officer there the whole time I was in there?''

''Couple of 'em.''

''Why? Was I under arrest? I wasn't the driver. I was the victim.''

''It was for your protection, Mali,'' Dad finally said.

Alvin was quiet but I could hear him moving restlessly in the seat behind me. I tried to turn around to look at Dad but the cast made it impossible. I gazed at Tad, who was driving as if he were on a minibike in the fast lane of the Jersey Turnpike.

"What's going on?" I asked.

"We'll talk when we get home," he said.

The ride was short but so quiet I didn't know if we were coming from or going to a funeral.

chapter

nineteen

Ruffin was so glad to see me he nearly bowled me over. His wagging tail beat against me with the force and power of a hammer, and all the pain I thought I'd left in the hospital came back. I hobbled over to the sofa and eased down against the pillows. Alvin shooed him back to his favorite spot near the fireplace while Dad made sure I was comfortable. Everyone busied themselves with small activity and my patience faded as I watched.

"What. The. Hell. Is. Going. On?"

I try not to use hard language in Alvin's presence but my patience was gone and something else, fear perhaps, had settled in its space. Tad turned. He had been checking the windows, making sure they were locked. Now he came over to sit next to me.

"Mali. Here's what happened. The hit-and-run was no accident."

"What?"

"It was deliberate."

My mind scrambled with images, memory. Was it someone from the precinct where I'd filed the lawsuit? The cop who'd harassed me, made all those threatening phone calls, was now dead. Terry Keenan had been killed in a crack den uptown. He and Danny Williams, Tad's partner, had been part of a drug distribution network, and Danny had shot Terry in that small room just as the DEA busted in. I had been trapped in there and saw the whole thing.

Was someone at the precinct still nursing some misplaced grudge because two of their own had been brought down and the entire precinct had come under a cloud?

"How do you know it was deliberate?" I asked. "Who was it?"

"James."

"James?"

I stared at him. James. When it finally registered, I wanted to laugh but the side of my face still felt as if I'd run into a wall. James. The coward couldn't deal face-to-face. He had to use a car to get at me.

"I had the car impounded," Tad said. "It had been stolen and his prints came up along with some others, plus when he jumped out of the wreck, several witnesses got a pretty good look as he ran."

Alvin rose suddenly from the chair where he'd been listening quietly. "If me and my boys find him, Mali, he's gonna get tagged. He's gonna wish he'd picked someone else to mess over. I got Morris and Clarence on the drum too. We'll get him."

I watched him pace the floor, his long legs covering the length of the room in what seemed like five steps, his muscular arms pressed against his chest. His dark handsome face had lost its softness. He was about to say more when Dad held up his hand.

"Alvin, that man is crazy and he's dangerous. I understand how you feel but I'm asking you not to get involved. And I'm asking you not to involve Morris or Clarence either."

"But, Grandpa, he meant to kill—"

"That's true but you've got to let the police handle this."

Alvin shot a glance at Tad, a scowl that said if the cops were doing their job, how come they haven't found him yet?

"We'll get him," Tad said, acknowledging the unspoken question.

Alvin glared at him, then looked at me again. "See, Mali. If Aunt Celia was here, she'd know how to take care of business. She wouldn't wait for anything or anybody. They'd just slow her down."

With that he turned and walked out of the room. His footsteps echoed loudly on the stairs, then we listened to his bedroom door slam shut.

Dad cleared his throat and rose to move toward the stairs. "That boy is gettin' beside himself. He needs to—"

"No, Mr. Anderson. Wait," Tad said. "Leave him alone for a while. He's more frightened for Mali than he is angry. He feels we're not doing enough but we'll get James. We will get him."

Dad nodded but his face looked drawn.

"Who's his Aunt Celia?" Tad asked.

"Actually, it's my grandaunt," I said. "She was my mother's aunt. Lived in Charleston in the twenties and had her own way of dealing with things . . . Her boy was murdered by a cop for sitting on his own stoop."

And I told the story the way my mother had told it to me, the one story in particular that she had carried through the years like a shield on her arm and a rock in her pocket. I told it now to pull my mind away from the pain that was piercing my leg like a bullet.

"Celia was a medicine woman and went one night to help a midwife with a hard delivery. While she was helping to coax one stubborn child into the world, her own was taken out.

"It went like this, her neighbor said, who had watched from the shadows of her own porch. 'Saw the whole thing. Policeman, that big ugly one, come 'round the way, spotted Sun, and told 'im to move. Sun tell him he live in the house.

Ugly policeman, you know the one I'm talkin' about, said he didn't care. Wanted the boy off the steps by the time he made the corner again.

" 'And naturally Sun, bein' the boy he was raised to be, didn't move and the policeman when he made the corner again, came and tooken 'im away. We didn't know where and by the time we got word to Miss Celia, it was probably too late.'

"When Celia and Mr. Mickey, the colored undertaker, retrieved the broken body from the alley in back of the courthouse, she said not one word, other than what she instructed Mr. Mickey to do.

" 'No. Don't clean nuthin' on him. Leave him, leave his clothes just as you see it now. But you and your boys bring me the finest, the most beautiful box you have. I'll take care of everything else. Everything, you hear me?'

"And Mr. Mickey, knowing Celia, knew better than to say a word. So her boy, not quite eighteen, was laid in a velvet-lined casket of African mahogany, placed in the front parlor near the windows for two days with two rows of candles, and for two nights Aunt Celia sat with him in a cloud of frankincense.

"On the third sunrise, she placed a gold coin on each eyelid, and at his feet, a small hen, the red just beginning to dampen its white feathers, and she closed and sealed the casket herself.

"When Mr. Mickey arrived, she said, 'Too bad you colored and that police is white.'

"Mr. Mickey nodded and loaded the casket onto the horse-drawn carriage, knowing that in seven days the white undertaker would have someone knocking on his door.

"And sure enough, that cop making his rounds a week later fell to his knees and sucked his last breath right in front of Celia's stoop."

Tad nodded politely but I continued. He needed to hear the entire story in order to understand Alvin's attitude.

"Her prices doubled after that," I said. "Folks even came from out of state and she charged triple for court appearances. One time she waived her fee when a farmer had beaten a white boy for 'interfering' with his little girl.

"The farmer, looking ancient with his skin turned ashen from despair, sat in the first row, his head bowed before the judge, wondering what his new life would be like dragging an ankle chain. If they decided not to hang him.

"When the case was called, Celia walked in, gliding silently down the aisle. The court took a look at the little gauze bags pinned to her lapels—white bags no larger than postage stamps on the left, and blue bags, even smaller, on the right. One look and the judge, the jury, and the aggrieved plaintiff stampeded through the window, cleared the porch, and disappeared across the lawn.

" 'Miss Celia, how much I owe you?'

"And she had looked at the light that had come back in the farmer's eyes and then gazed at his terrified little girl and said, 'Nuthin'. Wasn't no trial.' "

Tad looked at me and shook his head. "You've got quite a family," he murmured.

I heard the skepticism and ignored it, but Dad said, "That's a true story. Part of our family history." He rose from the chair and strode up the stairs. "Let me see if Alvin's calmed down."

We listened until the footsteps faded and Tad said, "Kid's got a strong back."

I said nothing, wondering if it had been a good idea to have told Alvin about Aunt Celia.

"Does Elizabeth know it was James?"

"No. She probably dislikes him as much as you do, and I'd rather keep this under my cap for now. At least until we nail him."

In the quiet, I could hear the tick of the grandfather clock at the foot of the stairs. Tad shifted on the sofa and I heard him clear his throat. "There's something else," he said. "I rushed away from you that night because of a call . . ."

"What happened?"

"Felicia Temple was killed."

I stared at him. "Felicia? The artist?"

He nodded. "She'd been dead three days. The house-keeper had been away, and when she returned that Saturday, she found her in the kitchen."

The kitchen. I did not have to ask how she was killed. I closed my eyes, picturing what had been found on her body.

"This makes three now," he said.

Even as he said it, I had trouble ingesting it. Felicia Temple. Alone in that huge brownstone since the death of her husband more than five years ago. She was so attractive everyone had wondered how soon she'd remarry but she never did. Instead she'd devoted herself to her art, turning out one magnificent painting after another, and enough pieces of sculpture to fill a small museum.

In fact, her house *was* a museum, an art gallery, and a sculpture studio all rolled in one and had been prominently featured on the Harlem house tour last spring.

She had a remarkable sense of humor. When the first strand of gray appeared, she had stripped all the color from her hair and dyed it an eye-popping silver.

"You can't beat Mother Nature," she'd said, "so the wisest thing to do is to work with her. Enhance her gifts. And have fun doing it. Laugh. Once we stop laughing, it's all over."

That's what she'd told Dad when he'd attended one of her in-house exhibits. He'd bought one of her sculptures, a twenty-inch statue of an African warrior carved from lignum vitae in the shape of a sword, his shoulders jutting out like the haft and his arms vanishing into his sides to form the blade. A coil of metal encircled his neck and a five-inch helmet of sharply pointed brass extended from his head.

Dad had placed it on the mantel and stared at its fierce expression, trying to think of a name for it. "Felicia said 'lignum vitae' means wood of life and is one of the hardest

woods in the world. Well, this is one hard, tough-lookin'
brother. Gotta find a suitable title. Wouldn't want him mad at
me for misnaming him.''

"Why don't you ask Felicia?" I'd said.

Instead, he'd asked her out to dinner. In fact they'd gone
out several times and I'd entertained the idea of having a
stepmother only ten years older than I was and it seemed like
a good idea. Dad had been a widower long enough. But nothing happened. They'd remained good friends and she'd remained single and so had he.

Now she was gone and now I understood the desolation in
back of the unshed tears when Dad looked at me.

"Listen," I said as Tad rose and moved toward the bar.
"Fix me a double Absolut. No ice."

"You sure? What about your pain medication?"

"I'm not taking it. Makes me too sleepy."

I watched him standing at the bar, uncapping the bottles,
pouring my drink, and pouring his own, and I wondered what
Felicia'd been doing in her last moments. How had the killer
surprised her? How had he gotten in the house? Claudine.
Marie. Felicia. How had they been so trusting?

Tad handed me the glass but now I felt a constriction in
my throat and lost my desire for the drink. I studied the clear
liquid, thinking of the cereal scattered over the bodies.

"What happened with the videotape?" I asked, trying to
clear the images from my mind.

Tad came to sit near me again. "The film was shot outside
the supermarket on 130th Street, just as Billy described, and

the hands were there, definitely working on the box of cereal, but when I tried for a possible ID the manager wasn't too cooperative. Asked for a warrant 'cause he didn't want to end up on the wrong end of a lawsuit. I got the warrant but meanwhile one of the employees had split.''

''Who?''

''Guy who'd been working off the books, no Social Security number, address someplace in the Bronx. Went up there and found a vacant lot. In fact, the whole block had been knocked down. New construction going up all around Prospect. Street guy told me the spot had been vacant about two years. So I'm back to square one.''

''You're back to Harlem,'' I said. ''I think he's right here, somewhere in the neighborhood. Felicia, Marie, Claudine. All were roughly in the same area so I think the guy's around here too. Were you able to get a description?''

''Guy was also vague about that. He was more worried about covering his own back than he was about somebody stealing a box of cereal. Store's part of a chain but independently managed and he may be skimming.

''Anyway, he said that the guy was about five feet eleven, not too well developed, but arms like he's into weights. Brown complexion, perpetual frown, mid-twenties, close-cut hair. Goes by the nickname Ache. But he couldn't ID the hands. Said it could be anyone and he was going to beef up security. He was nervous as hell. Probably thinks I'm gonna call the Department of Labor to come in and scan his books.''

I shrugged and leaned back on the sofa. The manager was

right. It could be anyone. I'd shopped at several stores on sale days and saw guys who'd wandered in off the street to bag groceries just for tips. Grown men. Trying to survive in hard times.

Frustration etched the curve of Tad's mouth as he paced the floor just as Alvin had done earlier. Not only was he trying to chase down a madman but he was confronted with my problem with James as well.

"Why don't you let someone else in the squad look for James?" I said. "You're handling a tough enough case as it is."

He stopped moving long enough to look at me. "Mali, I should've put you in a cab. But I left you alone on a corner. I rushed off without even thinking. This is my fault and I have to take care of it. See it doesn't happen again."

I raised my glass then and tried to take a sip but the stuff was too strong. My cough was so deep it scared me into putting the glass down. Then the dull throb in my hip and leg which I'd tried to ignore had moved beyond mere aching. Geniune pain was back.

"You all right?"

"I don't know. This news about Felicia. About James. So much stuff has happened and I feel as if I've been away, hiding out somewhere."

I leaned back against the cushions and studied Tad's face. Frustration seemed to deepen the lines around his mouth, and his eyes—his flecked pupils normally so intense—now seemed dull and shallow. This problem was affecting him more deeply than I realized. I searched through the tangle of circumstance for something, anything, that might be helpful.

"Did you know that Felicia and my dad once dated?"

"He mentioned it, but didn't go into details, except to say he'd bought a sculpture from her."

"There it is," I said, pointing to the mantel. The statue wavered as my vision blurred and suddenly I was crying and couldn't stop. It wasn't the pain in my arm or leg that caused my outcry, although that was pretty bad. This was a different injury, knowing that I would never see or hear or speak to any of these women again.

He leaned forward, gathering me to him. "Listen, Mali. I'm sorry. This was a lot to lay on you all at once. You need to relax, get some sleep."

We looked at the stairs and knew I couldn't make it past the first step, so I stretched out on the sofa and he spread a light blanket over me.

"I'll sit here awhile in case you need anything," he whispered. He settled in the chair and closed his eyes. I knew he was not asleep, but thinking of a madman, a serial killer on the loose, with no idea where or when he would strike again.

chapter

twenty

"Haven't seen you in a while. How've you been?"

"Okay," Ache whispered as the waitress wiped the counter in front of him and placed a napkin and silverware near his right elbow. He leaned forward, carefully studying the menu, wondering what three dollars could buy. Pan Pan's had good food but for him it always came down to the same thing: a bowl of soup, a cup of tea, and possibly one of those home-baked biscuits, if he left a smaller tip.

The waitress lingered a minute, then moved to wait on someone else. Ache glanced around at the signs on the wall advertising the specials, and below the signs, the row of heavy waffle irons that sent out the sweet, steaming aroma every time a lid was lifted.

The few times he ate here, he always sat on the end seat at the counter in the back. This way, he could scan the whole place. The only people he couldn't see were the guys in the kitchen behind the high partition in back of him but he could hear their voices, hear the clatter of plates and brief and busy exchanges as the waitresses picked up the dishes. Other than that, he could see everybody. This made him comfortable.

He stared beyond the print on the menu, adrift in his thoughts.

Pass up those waffles. Ain't no good anyway with all that syrup and mile-high pile a fried chicken stacked on top. Like the last meal before they strap you in the chair.

He glanced at an old man sitting several seats away. Most of the man's front teeth were missing but he had tucked his napkin determinedly under his chin, preparing to tackle the grits-eggs-and-country-bacon special along with the side of toast soaking up the butter and jelly.

Damn!

He stared at the man's plate, then lowered his head again and focused on the menu so that he wouldn't have to look at the abundance surrounding him.

Three days. Three days I ain't worked. No more money. And

all 'cause a that gray-eyed bitch. Starin' right through me just like Mercy Anne but she saw me. She sent that cop. I knew he was The Man before he even flipped his shield. I knew it.

He had left the box of orange juice he'd been stacking, abandoned it in front of the frozen food case and hurried to the bathroom, then walked quickly through the loading area in the back of the store where he dodged noisy hi-los shifting and stacking cartons and boxes into cardboard mountains. Once outside, he had edged between the two double-parked tractor trailers, scooted across the street, and never looked back.

Wasn't nobody but her sent him. Made me lose my job. Lose my job.

The waitress was standing over him again with the order pad in her hand. "You ready, sir?"

He nodded. Nobody had ever called him "sir" except for the few times he'd come in here.

"Yeah. Uh, how's the soup today?" he asked, knowing the answer before she opened her mouth. Of course it was good. What else was she going to say, but he needed to prolong the moment.

"It's pretty good." She smiled, tapping the pencil against the pad. "Navy bean or pea soup. Which would you like?"

"It don't matter. And a side order of biscuits and a cup of tea."

"Thank you." She smiled again and moved away to take another order and he felt disappointed that she hadn't called him "sir" again. He followed the music of her voice, listened carefully, and heard her call some of the others "sweetie," "honey," and "baby."

Mmmhmph. She ain't called me that. What the fuck's goin' on? Okay. That the way you wanna play? On again, off again? Then no tip for your ass, bitch!

The large bowl was placed before him, navy bean, thick and fragrant. And heavy enough to hold him until he could figure out his next move. He brought the spoon to his mouth and thought of the homeless man who'd held the door open for him when he'd entered the restaurant. He'd ignored the filthy outstretched palm but saw it now as he stirred the soup.

Bullshit! Ain't gonna happen. Out on the street. Unh-unh, not me.

He thought of the vendors outside cluttering the side-walk, waiting for the stream of potential buyers to emerge from the subway.

Now, sellin' stuff. That'd be all right. Be my own boss. In business for myself. Don't have to think about kissin' nobody's ass. Just hi and good-bye. You don't like what I'm sellin', keep steppin'. . . Yeah, that be kinda nice.

He tasted the soup, imagining his booming business: scarves, socks, batteries, Krazy Glue, barrettes. Stuff people needed. And when he got hungry, he could leave someone else in charge—an assistant maybe—somebody who knew better than to steal if they knew what was good for them— leave him outside raking up dollars while he strolled in where it was nice and warm and everybody smiling, calling him "sir." And he'd treat himself to a full dinner including dessert, then leave a tip so large they'd talk about it for days . . .

He felt better and the soup tasted pretty good when he swallowed.

But where the guys cop their stuff from? How much it cost? What if I can't get a spot on the corner? Crowded as it is, they might run me off. "No more room, dammit. Find someplace else to squat."

"Aw no! You steppin' on toes now! Steppin' on toes! . . . The fuck you comin' off at? This corner's free! You ain't paid for shit. That's right! Fuck you and your mama too. One a these days I'm a have all a y'all kissin' my black ass!"

He looked up. The waitress had turned, her pad and pencil frozen in midair. The clerk at the takeout counter and several customers were staring. One of the cooks—a man with fists like southern hams—had stepped from behind the high counter in back of him. Even the homeless man had cupped his hand against the glass and was peering inside. All staring.

He looked down. The bowl was empty and the biscuits were gone from the saucer.

"Somebody stole 'em! I don't remember eatin' 'em! Everybody lookin', goddammit, and nobody seen who stole my stuff? What the fuck's goin' on?"

He rose abruptly and snatched up the check lying beside his glass.

Who put it there? How long was it there? Fuck it, he didn't

care. He was leaving anyway. And someday when he returned, he'd be rolling in dollars and they'd be damn glad to
see him. Glad to see the biggest goddamn tip ever laid on this
counter.

Once outside, the cool air hit him in the face and the rage
ebbed as quickly as it had come. The beat above his eyebrow
slowed and the pounding fist in his chest eased. He lingered,
taking in the hum of activity as people emerged from the
subway. He watched a teenager selling umbrellas and another
vendor who had a low flatbed of packaged strawberries, oranges, and tomatoes which seemed to sell themselves.

That's easy. I could do that.

He moved around the crowd and waited at the corner for
the light to change.

*I could do that. First, I got to take care a some business on
Strivers' Row. Ain't seen not even her shadow for nearly three
weeks now. Maybe she away. (Maybe she ain't real.) Ha! Like
that last one, like Mercy Anne. Look right through me like I was
nuthin'. Invisible. Well, she gonna be nuthin' when I get to her
neck. She be nuthin'.*

He jammed his hands in his pockets and walked across
Malcolm X Boulevard, past the open courtyard near the Y
where the sign against the back wall announced in faded letters: "Harlem Plays the Best Ball in the Country." On the
corner of Adam Clayton Powell Boulevard, he gazed at the

sealed windows of the old Smalls Paradise, then he quickened his steps and headed uptown.

Maybe she ain't even real.

What you sayin' she ain't real? She make you lose your job. That's real, ain't it?

He walked past a knot of children laughing over a hop-scotch game, past two women sitting on a stoop near the Pretty City Cocktail Lounge, one rocking a baby stroller to rap lyrics flowing from a parked Lincoln Navigator where a man was cleaning the interior.

The jingle of a Mister Softee truck drifted on the breeze but he did not see or hear or feel any of this. He walked in the fading light fingering in his pocket an old-fashioned single-edge barber's instrument honed on a bluestone to a fine edge.

No wire this time. This time I wanna see her face. Ring that bell and watch her eyes. She open the door, bring the blade across those goddamn eyes. No wire this time. The last thing she gonna see is me.

chapter

twenty-one

I always wondered what it felt like to be in lockdown and now I knew. I was housebound, although my hip, knee, and arm were almost functional thanks to the every-other-day visits by the physical therapist. The first few days of exercise had been a test, but lately, though the pain was still there, I wasn't gritting my teeth so audibly.

I was still wearing the brace but I wanted to feel the pavement under my feet, take in a movie, dine at a restaurant, walk Ruffin, watch Alvin and Clarence and Morris play ball.

Sit in on Dad's jazz sessions at the Club Harlem. Most of all, I wanted to curl up with Tad on his terrace and watch the moon light up the Harlem River.

But before I did any of that, I wanted to find James and kick his sorry butt from here to Jersey and then stomp his remains into the mud of the Meadowlands.

Even if I couldn't raise my foot without groveling in pain, even if I wound up breaking my leg again, I wanted to do it.

But Dad had put his own foot down. "You refused police protection, so stay in. At least till James is caught."

"It might take a year to find him," I'd said.

He had looked at me then and shrugged. "So that means you'll live a year longer."

The upside to my imprisonment was the chance to sift through a mountain of accumulated paperwork and start on my reading list for classes that would begin in the fall. I piled all that stuff around me and lay on the sofa, busily staring at the ceiling when the phone rang.

"Mali? I'm coming right over."

"Elizabeth? What's up, girl?"

"Be there in a minute. I want to see your face when I tell you."

She hung up, leaving me to quickly gather all of the books and papers in a neat pile so she'd have someplace to sit and also to wonder if she'd gotten engaged and, if so, what was the size of the rock on her finger and eventually what color my maid of honor's gown was likely to be.

She must have had a cab waiting in her lobby because I barely finished fluffing the pillows when the bell rang.

I made my way to the door and she stood there smiling.

"Are congrats in order?" I asked.

"Depends on you," she said, stepping into the foyer and bringing with her a rush of air, fresh and free and summery and making me more aware than ever of my incarceration.

Her pale blue linen suit set off the navy silk blouse, and her auburn shoulder-length locks were bundled at the back of her neck, held there by a thin strip of blue and white kente cloth. She made her way into the living room balancing perfectly on three-inch black patent heels. I stomped behind her in my brace, executing a credible imitation of Captain Ahab.

She settled onto the sofa and rested her attaché case on the coffee table. "Studying?" she asked, looking at the pile of material.

"Thinking about it," I sighed.

"Well, think about this. The department has finally made an offer I think you can live with."

"What kind?"

"Reinstatement at the rank of detective first grade, back pay at that level for the time you were off the job, and immediate retirement on ninety percent disability."

"I'm not disabled," I said, hobbling to the chair to sit down. "What are they basing the disability on?"

"Post-traumatic stress stuff. I emphasized the fact that you'd been held hostage in that crack den by two of New

York's Finest, that they'd intended to kill you to cover their tracks. They do not want the memory of that incident resurrected under any circumstances."

"Which is exactly what'll happen if the case goes to trial," I said. "They know I'll open my big mouth and it'll be a media circus."

Elizabeth rose from the sofa to fix herself a drink. I sipped soda.

"Right now, Mali, they're under the gun, what with Johnnie Cochran taking over the Abner Louima case in Brooklyn. And Mrs. Baez in the Bronx crusading in memory of her son. And there's also the incident where a young man was handcuffed and held naked in the hallway while the boys in blue wrecked his apartment, even though it was the wrong apartment. And before they took him down to the precinct, they forced him to dress in women's clothing . . ."

I shook my head, listening to this litany of abuse and wondering when and if things would ever change. The department was slapped with a lawsuit every other week and no one seemed interested in reining these officers in—the few bad apples, as they liked to say.

The apples were infecting the entire system, rotting it away, and the administration seemed only interested in damage control after the damage had been done. Millions were draining from the city treasury when the hole could've been plugged by weeding out the misfits early on.

The problem was that the ones doing the hiring favored those who looked and acted just like them. Protect and serve.

Protect your ass and serve yourself with the largest helping of drug dollars on the planet.

I was drowning in the well of memory, falling deeper into the ugliness of the past, when Elizabeth interrupted.

"If you're not disabled, you damn sure will be soon," she said quietly. "You should see your face, girl. You're going to develop an ulcer the size of Manhattan if you go on like ths. You say you're not disabled but I think you are, in some way. You're hauling memory around like a two-ton weight. Anger is like acid. It'll eat you alive. You gotta let it go. Please, Mali."

She leaned over to tap my hand. "Listen, we've already lost one of our crowd, and Deborah in Washington, for all intents and purposes, is practically a borderline basket case. I don't want to see you in a padded cell or have to bring flowers up to Woodlawn if you . . ."

I glanced at her and saw that her normally clear eyes had darkened and her finely shaped brows were gathered almost in the center of her forehead. Her voice, which could sound so formidable on cross-examination, now seemed to falter.

I closed off my own feelings: my anger at the department, the anger I felt toward James, the smothering sense of loss that overwhelmed me when I thought of Claudine, Marie, and Felicia. And the vague feeling that whoever was doing this probably had someone else already targeted.

Elizabeth was right. Somehow I had to let go of everything. Settling the suit was the first step.

"Let me talk it over with Dad when he comes in. See

what he thinks. A detective first grade draws a pretty decent salary. Right now it sounds like a pretty good offer."

That brought a smile to Elizabeth's face and her brows relaxed. "Well, you stood your ground and didn't back down. I'm damn proud of you. When this is over, we're gonna pop a whole case of bubbly."

"Speaking of which, how about another cocktail?"

"Can't. Expecting a client in an hour. How's the therapist working out?"

"Fine. Straightening out knots and kinks I didn't know I had, except I don't know when I'll be free of this brace."

"Mali, be thankful it wasn't any worse. That first day in the hospital, I looked at you and . . ." She shifted on the edge of the sofa and her voice changed again. "You know I'm no good at prayer, but I prayed that night until morning and then every night afterward."

"Knowing that means a lot to me," I said, reaching for her hand. "Thank you." I had planned to tell her finally that it was James who had nearly killed me, but changed my mind. She was upset enough.

"How's David?" I asked, changing the subject.

Now her eyes regained their color and she was smiling broadly. "He's getting better by the day, but that's another story for another day."

She glanced at her watch and took a sheaf of papers out of her case. "Gotta go but I'll stop by tomorrow. I've outlined everything. Cross out whatever you disagree with and we can discuss it. They want an answer within ten days."

I glanced up from the thick packet she handed me. "Ten days? After three years, they now want an answer in ten days?"

"Mali, you know how the system works," Elizabeth sighed, gathering her bag. "It's held together by Krazy Glue and run by folks who're inhaling it."

chapter

twenty-two

Our rear garden is probably small enough to fit (with room to spare) inside one of Martha Stewart's small henhouses, but in my confinement, my appreciation for this tiny crowded patch of Eden had grown daily by sizable increments.

I suddenly admired the rear wall, though the only visible work of art was the out-of-control ivy spreading like a green plague. I found belated comfort in one of the two Adirondack chairs, its wood worn and scratched but still serviceable after years of benign neglect.

I reacquainted myself with the beauty and utility of the terra-cotta planters where Dad and Alvin cultivated cherry tomatoes and strawberries and where I'd promised to pitch in year after year but never got around to doing anything except maybe to eat the fruits of their labor.

Two days ago, when I was able to maneuver down the three steps to the garden, I'd settled in one of the chairs, thankful for the sight of the drifting clouds overhead, the music of the birds as they helped themselves to the strawberries, and thankful that the garden had saved me from breaking down like a con in a late-night grade Z prison movie.

This feeling now dissolved, ingrate that I was, as I stood on the front steps watching Elizabeth, shoulder bag in one arm and attaché in the other, walk toward Seventh Avenue. She did not have to think twice about James crawling out of a hole and surprising her.

She disappeared around the corner and I forgot about the reading and went to the backyard to sit on the steps and stare at the tomatoes. I was plotting a way to get out without Dad threatening to chain me to the radiator when I heard the front door close and Alvin's quick footsteps on the stairs. A minute later he was running back down.

I pushed myself up from the steps. I could not run, and by the time I walked through the house, he was out the door. I leaned on the railing, my leg aching from the sudden effort, and called after him. "Where're you going?"

He turned to face me but kept walking backward, putting distance between us.

"Play some ball," he said, pointing to the bat he carried. He waved and disappeared around the corner onto Seventh Avenue. I shooed Ruffin back inside and headed toward the garden again, but the bell rang. Ruffin's bark didn't discourage the caller and I stood in the middle of the hallway, deciding whether to answer.

When I opened the door again, Clarence and Morris were staring at me, wide-eyed and out of breath.

"Miss Mali, is Alvin here?"

"He just left a minute ago," I said. "Said he was going to play ball. Is . . . something the matter?"

"Well," said Morris, leaning on one foot then the other, "it's like . . ."

"Naw, Morris. This ain't no time for slow dancin'," Clarence said, tapping him on the arm. "We gotta step to it."

"What? What happened?"

"Miss Mali. We found out where James is."

"What?"

"He's holed up right there in 136th Street. And that's where Alvin's headed. Said he's gonna take care a him."

My knees were about to give way but I held onto the wall and made my way to the phone. Dad was downtown, shopping for a new jacket, and I had no idea what store he'd gone to.

James was on 136th Street. I couldn't believe it. Right under Maxie's nose. I found the small tray on the bar where I'd dropped Miss Dottie's phone number and prayed that she'd be home when I dialed.

She came on sounding out of breath. "Wanted to pick up before the machine came on," she said. "People hear a machine, they hang up. Oh, yeah, I remember. You the gray-eyed girl, Jeffrey Anderson's daughter. You were lookin' for James. How you doin'? Found him yet?" Morris and Clarence had now stepped inside, waiting, and I glanced at them.

"I know where James is," I said, "and I want Maxie to get to him before my nephew does. The boy is only twelve years old and he's no match for James. He's on his way there now."

"Only twelve?" I heard the outtake of her breath. "The boy got brass, that's for sure, but say the word. I can get to Maxie."

I handed the phone to Clarence. "Tell her where James is."

"He's in his old stompin' grounds, 'cept now he's squattin' in an abandoned building and only comes out at night . . ."

"To steal," Morris said. "Tell her he's in that gray house next to the funeral parlor with the awning, the one in the middle of the block. Crackerjack, the crackhead named Jackie, come in the park. She asked for two dollars and told us what we wanted to know . . ."

"Right under Maxie's nose," I said.

Morris looked at me. "You mean he dodgin' Maxie too? Dang. That's deep!"

Clarence handed the phone to me again and I listened to Miss Dottie's heavy breathing. "Don't worry, Mali. I'm gettin' on the drum right now. I'll take care of it. Your nephew'll be all right. What's his name?"

"Alvin. He's medium height, dark brown, wearing a white T-shirt, and he's carrying a baseball bat."

"Don't worry," she said again, and the phone went dead.

I called Tad but there was no answer. I called the squad room at the precinct and the machine said that he was in a meeting. I beeped him, left a message, then struggled to collar Ruffin. Brace or no brace, I was going to 136th Street even if I had to travel on Ruffin's back.

At Powell Boulevard Clarence stepped into the street with his hand held high. He whistled, waved, and finally yelled at the procession of gypsy cabs who slowed momentarily, then pumped the pedal to weave back into the stream of traffic.

"Morris," Clarence yelled, "step back with Ruffin. We can hike but Miss Mali gotta cab it."

As he spoke, a yellow cab halted a few feet away and discharged two passengers, tourists complete with cameras and maps. They hesitated and looked around and I wondered if they were preparing to don pith helmets.

The man smiled and waved to Clarence.

The woman, lean as an athlete, with short-cut hair the color of sand, bent toward her companion, a blunt-looking young man with tiny square glasses perched dangerously on the tip of his nose. They conferred in a language none of us could decipher. Was it Dutch? Flemish? Croatian? We heard four English words—"block of hard workers." They looked at us and waited, smiling expectantly.

"If you lookin' for Strivers' Row," Clarence said, "this is it."

He stepped toward the cab before they closed the door but the off-duty sign flashed on and the cabbie sped away with a shimmying fishtail that left the smell of burning rubber in the air. The maneuver slammed the door shut, leaving all of us, tourists and locals together, staring.

"I seen 'em get outta Dodge but never like that," Clarence murmured.

We left the tourists and walked. Even with the pain pill, and with Morris holding Ruffin's leash and Clarence holding me, it took nearly fifteen minutes to navigate three and a half blocks. The last half-block was the worst and my leg felt as if I had walked through fire.

At 136th Street we stood watching the rotating lights of an ambulance fade down the block and across Malcolm X Boulevard.

Alvin. Where was Alvin? There was no one in sight and the silence was stunning. No one was sitting on a stoop, or lounging in a doorway, or walking by. What had happened?

Clarence and Morris also gazed up and down the block, shrugging and whispering in the unnatural silence.

My nerves disintegrated and I collapsed against a car, convinced that Alvin had confronted James and James had somehow managed to get the bat away and had used it on him.

"Miss Dottie would know." My voice broke the silence and I grabbed Clarence's arm. We limped to the middle of the block and I tried not to let my imagination run wild. I had never seen this or any other block in Harlem so quiet. I pointed to her house and Morris rang the bell. She opened the door and Alvin was standing behind her. In the rose glow of the overhead lamp, his face looked ruddy, almost wholesome in the dim light, but I saw the shaking in his shoulders.

"Take the child home, Mali. He seen too much tonight." Miss Dottie's voice was a hoarse whisper afloat in the silence.

Alvin stepped away from the light and I looked closely. His eyes were half closed and an ashy tinge had broken through the deep brown of his coloring.

"Alvin, you all right?"

"I'm . . . fine. Let's go." He turned to Miss Dottie and hugged her. "Thanks, ma'am. I mean it. Thanks . . ."

"That's all right, baby. You go get a good night's sleep and all this'll be behind you come tomorrow. It'll be just a bad dream."

I looked from one to the other and asked again, "What happened?"

Miss Dottie beckoned to me but I could no longer move. She saw the brace on my leg and came outside. Alvin had moved away to join Morris and Clarence. There were no high fives, only whispered conversation and Alvin pointing to the sealed house where the front door had been broken in.

"Maxie got 'im," Miss Dottie said. "Sent his callin' cards, Eeny, Meanie, Miney, and Moe, into the building."

"Who're they?"

"You mean what're they. Those are his pit bulls. Four of 'em. First one got in and chased James out to the street where the other three was circlin'. I peeped through the blinds and watched Maxie sittin' right over there on that stoop." She pointed across the street. "Loungin' there the whole time, flingin' all that hair out his eyes, and drawin' on the fattest blunt you ever seen. And watchin' the whole thing.

"Nobody called the cops or ambulance or nuthin' 'cause they knew who those dogs belonged to and figured whoever was gettin' it probably deserved it. Maxie don't get dirty unless he figure you trying to play him.

"Dogs did a job. Ambulance finally came and picked up what was left but this is one time where the old line don't mean a thing." I nodded, knowing what the old line was. Harlem Hospital. "If you go in there squawkin', guaranteed you'll come out walkin'."

"Undertaker can try to fix him up a little but I bet his own mama'll have a time recognizin' him. Best thing is a closed casket."

"Did . . . Alvin see it?"

She shook her head. " 'Fraid so. Some of it, at least. He came down the block at the tail end of everything, so he probably saw the worst part. James was really spread out . . . I'm sorry I couldn't stop 'im from seein' that, Mali. I'm sorry."

I followed her glance down the street and saw the bits and pieces of stained clothing. She touched my shoulder and then handed me a tissue. I didn't know if I had started to cry because Alvin had witnessed it, or because I knew what Claudine and Marie had suffered. It was over. All the hard feeling I'd harbored was finally gone. James was gone.

But as they say, be careful what you wish for.

James was no longer here but Alvin saw him taken out. He had witnessed a bloodbath.

"You take it easy on that leg now, Mali," Miss Dottie said. "It looks kinda swollen to me. How'd you get that anyway?"

"James ran me down in a stolen car."

She looked at me and whispered, "Well, I'll be damned. I'll be damned."

We made our way back to Seventh Avenue to try to hail a cab again when Tad pulled up and the car's tinted window slid down. He parked, allowing me to slide into the backseat. Alvin now had Ruffin's collar.

"Listen," I said. "Why don't you and your boys walk Ruffin back to the house?"

He shook his head, still silent. A slight breeze caused his shirt to billow around his chest, making the shirt look large, as if it did not belong to him. I wanted to pull him into the car and cry with him in my arms, but he would never allow that. Not with his crew watching.

They walked away with Ruffin leading. I watched them: Clarence's tall thin frame overshadowing Morris and Alvin by a foot and a half and Morris's hair finely rolled into the thin locks his mother had only recently allowed him to cultivate. And Alvin, leading Ruffin, who had disobeyed Dad to try to settle a score the way he knew Aunt Celia would have done.

I watched until they were out of sight, then glanced at the bat Alvin had placed on the seat beside me, but I said nothing. I was too numb and words would not come.

Tad was quiet also. By the time we reached home, my leg was twice its normal size and he had to carry me inside where Dad was waiting.

Getting that brace off was like performing major surgery. I was glad that Morris and Clarence had gone home and Alvin was upstairs in his room and Tad had turned the stereo up louder than usual. I am no hero and I invented new words to describe James and hoped he heard them wherever Maxie had sent him.

chapter

twenty-three

The chime, soft as it was, jolted me. I opened my eyes and lay on the sofa, waiting for Ruffin to trot to the door. The bell sounded again and I realized in the silence that Dad had taken him out for his morning run.

Alvin came downstairs in his pajamas, rubbing the sleep from his eyes. When he opened the door, Elizabeth was outside, searching in her purse for her cell phone. She rushed past him, checked herself, and turned back to give him a peck on the cheek. "Sorry. Good morning, handsome. How're you doing?"

"Okay, I guess."

He said no more and we both watched him retreat up the stairs like a ghost. I swung my legs off the sofa as she entered the room, and when she saw me, she stopped short.

"Girl! What on earth? What happened to you?"

"I had a bad night," I said, waving her to a chair.

She pushed a copy of the *Daily Challenge* toward me but I pushed it away. "I know what it says," I whispered. "I was there."

Her expression changed and her voice dropped to a whisper. "Mali, for God's sake. What's going on?"

She leaned forward and her face resembled a wreath of frowns. But I looked at her crisp linen suit not yet affected by the heat of the day and I saw the beautiful black patent-leather shoes on her feet. I looked at them and wondered if I'd ever be able to walk again in similar shoes; or run with Ruffin in the park, or dance barefoot at midnight on the beach again with Tad. I thought of Alvin and how Dad and I had spent most of last night trying to figure out how best to deal with what the boy had seen. I thought of James and how I'd arrived at this point.

"How about some coffee?" I said. "Just switch on the machine in the kitchen. I'll take mine black."

She took off her jacket and a few minutes later returned and set a tray with two steaming cups of Jamaican Blue

Mountain coffee on the low table in front of the sofa. Then she settled into the chair opposite, waiting. I glanced at the paper near the tray and said, "You ever wondered why I disliked James? I mean from day one?"

"Disliked? Despised would be more accurate," she said, reaching for her cup and cradling it in her hands. "I always thought your feelings were too . . . intense, too discordant relative to what was happening to Claudine. Don't get me wrong. I hated what he'd done. And I hated the idea that what was happening was happening between two married people and it was hardly any of our business to interfere, but you . . . you seemed ready to cancel his contract every time you ran into him."

"Well, as it turned out, he ran into me."

"What?"

"That's right. That's how I ended up in the hospital. The incident last night was the culmination of a long, long mutual antagonism."

"What happened?"

I leaned back on the sofa and pressed my hand to my knee, trying to ignore the pain and trying not to look at the swelling. And I tried to keep my voice steady as I spoke: "James stepped out of line from day one. The day he and Claudine got married. At the reception."

Elizabeth put her cup down and shook her head. The auburn highlights in her locks caught the rays of the early sun and looked almost golden against her brown skin. She shook her hair again, scattering the light. Then she stared at me but remained silent, allowing me to go on.

"You remember the reception, high-octane crowd, everyone partying, the bubbly flowing, threatening to drown us all; Claudine looked so radiant, smiling for everyone. And the band even had the seniors on the floor strutting the electric slide.

"Well, too much bubbly had me ready to pee. I left the ballroom and walked down the hall to the bathroom. When I opened the door, James pushed in behind me . . ."

"Damn!"

"He came in with some damn slick talk, stepped up with a proposition, and I popped him in the mouth. He got crazy and tried to lock us both in there, saying no bitch was gonna get away with hitting him.

"Remember you'd asked me how the sleeve of my gown had gotten torn and I said I'd caught it on a nail in the ladies' room. Well, the nail was James. I didn't back up or shut up. I was ready to go one-on-one and let him know. When he saw that I meant business, he opened the door but not before he warned that if I ever mentioned it, he'd tell Claudine that I had tried to come on to him. Imagine. The damn band hadn't even cooled off from playing the wedding march and the son of a bitch is in the ladies' room coming on to his wife's maid of honor.

"He challenged me, dared me to go running to Claudine. Said she'd believe him before she'd believe me. Claudine had been Benin's friend. And almost like a sister to me. Whether she took my word or his, I wasn't ready to break up her marriage or our friendship. But I was so damn mad I sat out the rest of the party. Said I had a headache, said my feet hurt. Actually, everything inside me was hurting.

"That's why I avoided their company as much as I did. When it was unavoidable and he'd catch my eye, he'd stare in a way that implied we had a thing going; a look that said 'we're in something together.' "

Elizabeth put her hand to her head and sighed. "I remember now. Your face, your sour expression. More like you were coping with a toothache. I even asked what was wrong and you never answered. You never answered." She leaned back in the chair and drew a deep breath. "He was worse than I thought."

"Well, it gets even worse. A few weeks ago, we had a light confrontation outside the Lido. He was convinced I'd told Claudine about him. He also accused me of telling Marie something. Said I'd be hearing from him. And I did."

I pointed to my knee and my arm. "He's the cause of this. He's the reason a plainclothes policeman was posted outside my hospital room."

"But why didn't you say something, Mali?"

"To whom?"

Elizabeth leaned forward again and I saw the disappointment in her expression. "To me. To me. I'm your attorney and your friend, remember?"

"I know you are, but Tad wanted to keep quiet about the

hit-and-run at least until James was caught. As for the feud, I didn't want to pull you into it. I mean the whole thing was so damn bizarre. Imagine being propositioned, not by an old battle-scarred veteran of a twenty-year marriage, but I was hit on by an hour's-old bridegroom who had no idea what 'I do' meant.

"My head was spinning, I was so angry. And as he said, it would've been his word against mine. So it was better to keep quiet. I never even told Dad."

"And of course you never mentioned this to Tad?"

I looked at her. "Are you serious? You know how that man is. Remember how tight he'd gotten when I'd tried to help Kendrick, Bertha's brother? Remember Erskin Harding, Alvin's chorus director? I couldn't go through that stuff again."

Elizabeth drained her cup and rose to get a refill. When she returned, I continued.

"So James went undercover and Alvin found out where he was. He went looking for him but I got to someone first who was looking for him also."

"Well, whoever it was must've been pretty damn mad. The papers said James was torn to pieces."

I nodded, hoping she would not go into details. "James is gone," I said, "but Alvin saw what happened. I think he saw most of it. He's a good kid and Dad and I have to figure out how to keep this from affecting him. And," I said, pressing my knee, "I have to learn to use this leg again. I'm back to square one."

chapter

twenty-four

"What you mean you was mugged? By who?"

Ache did not answer. Hazel clicked the remote and Jerry Springer shrank to a white dot and the screen went blank. The boxing match could wait. This was serious, this possibility of not having her money when she needed it. She turned on the lamp near the sofa, illuminating the sagging cushions, the paint-flaked walls, and floors that had not seen a mop since the linoleum was laid, years ago.

Hazel had once complained to her caseworker that she

needed a homemaker and one had come last year but didn't bother to take off her coat. She took one look and backed out the door, declaring that she had stopped doing hog pens when she left Tennessee.

When Hazel complained again, the caseworker had sighed, "You have an able-bodied relative, Ms. Milton, a son living with you who should be willing to help you with your household responsibilities."

She had stressed "responsibilities" as she looked around the living room and remained standing near the door, tapping one foot then the other to prevent something from crawling up her leg.

Once outside in the hallway, she'd shaken her coat and scarf and briefcase in an effort to deroach the articles before heading back to the office.

That was a year ago and Hazel only called sporadically to curse her out now. She was too involved in the drama of make-believe to think about responsibilities.

Now here was something else to distract her. She looked at her son standing stiffly in the doorway, as if he wasn't sure he still lived there.

"So what you gonna do about it? You was mugged but I still need my money. Life goes on, you know. What you gonna do?"

"I . . . can maybe ask for a loan. Yeah, a loan from the boss. See what he say . . ."

"You one dumb stupid—that boss ain't gonna give you the time of day. Might even fire your ass 'cause you was prob-

ably out there playin' Big Willie, flashin' your cash for everybody to see. No wonder somebody ripped you off, you dumb
sommabitch. You out a week's pay and I don't get nuthin'.
Well, you still sleepin' here and still usin' my toilet paper so
you owe me, you understand? You double up next week and I
don't wanna hear no shit about how you got tapped again,
you hear me?

"Put your money in your shoe next time. We ain't talkin'
no big-time dollars where it gon' have you walkin' with a
limp. That's what you shoulda done in the first damn place
but you didn't think of it 'cause you ain't got the brains you
was born with!"

She turned from him in disgust and pressed the remote
but a commercial was on, so she snapped the sound off, waving the control at arm's length like a maestro conducting a
difficult symphony.

Realizing she had probably missed a crucial point in
Jerry's show, her anger expanded, causing her to pull up a file
of memory to spread before her son and confirm how stupid
he really was.

"Can't even get a GED. Wanted to play basketball. How
was you gon' find the basket, dumb as you are? You'd lose
your way on the court. Two boys in your class, Pukie playin'
in the NFL and that other one, Tee, playin' basketball down
south somewhere. They big-time now. Seen Pukie on TV.
You, I see every day and ain't seen shit you done. 'Cept
maybe get uglier. Har, har . . ."

Ache shifted from one foot to the other, offering no defense. He was okay for at least another week, so it was all right for her to laugh, to slap her knee so hard the funk rose in a wave thick enough to choke him. It was okay. All he needed was probably another week. He'd take care of that little business on Strivers' Row and be gone. But he had no idea where he'd go. He couldn't think much beyond that, but he knew he was leaving. He had to leave. Find someplace else and start a new life. This time for good.

He'd passed Gray-Eyes' house enough times now to have their routine down to a science. But where was she?

Her father, or whoever he was—maybe her old man—he leave the house every Tuesday night with a bass. Limo show up at 7:30 on the dee-oh-tee. Must be big-time.

Sometimes he walk that horse, but there's somebody else in that house, kid who look like he don't take no shit. Left there the other night with a baseball bat. Trottin' off like he ready to do somebody in. And her callin' after him. Then two others come by. House like a fuckin' airport.

Then that nappy redhead with the high heels show up couple a times. Who's she? And that cop even step in, maybe askin' more questions. What was goin' on? Hell with him. Hell with 'em all. Make me lose my job, I'm a walk between all of 'em.

In the bedroom he turned on the fifteen-watt lamp but could not close his eyes. He stared at the cracks in the ceiling that spread like bleached veins through the peeling paint and concentrated on all the stuff that was happening to him.

Two guys right in my class got them scholarships, basketball, football. I couldn't get shit. Not even a piece of diploma. Two

weeks ago, couldn't even git to take the army test. And hadda
come back and listen to her tell me about it. "Be all you can
fuckin' be," she had laughed.

But that wasn't all . . .

He turned over, feeling the mattress cut into him like
gravel on an unpaved road, and thought of Hazel, and why he
had never been allowed to address her as "Mother" the way
other kids were able to call their mother.

"My name is Hazel! It ain't Ma, Mom, Mother. It ain't
none a that shit and don't you forget it," she had said when
he was old enough to mouth the word, and he had nodded
dumbly, the shock of the slap still ringing in his ears.

And the thing about his old man. What was going on? At
the recruitment center he didn't know his father's name and
they told him to come back with his birth certificate. He had
found it stuffed away in a rusted can in the kitchen cabinet.
He read it, examined it closely, and returned to the center,
where the officer handled it and then looked at him.

He was hoping the officer would discover a comma, a
hidden line, something in the murky bureaucratic phrasing, or
in the fine print, and he'd smile and explain and maybe
straighten out the puzzle. But the officer put his hand to his
mouth and coughed, then gazed at the paper again as if he'd
seen a lifetime of unthinkable things pass before him and
nothing made him blink anymore.

Hazel had been fifteen when he was born. Her father was
Nathan Milton, age thirty-eight according to the paper.

Ache's real name was Charles Milton, and according to the paper, his father was also Nathan Milton, age thirty-eight.

That can't be right.

Ache shook his head, still waiting for an answer when the officer handed him back the paper. His uniform was creased so sharply Ache wondered how he moved without cutting himself. He riffled through a packet of papers a second time, then said, "Where's your diploma? I don't see it here."

"I don't have none," Ache said, thinking of the paper he'd stuffed back in his pocket.

Can't fuckin' be right. Can't be. He held his breath, still waiting for the officer to explain.

"Okay. Your GED. We need to have your GED. Otherwise—"

But Ache was centered on the slip of paper in his pocket.

For three hours, he had wandered the periphery of Times Square trying to decide who should bear the weight of his discovery, feel the slit of the razor across the back, deep enough to divide muscle and bone, then melt, quick, into the crowd the way the manual said it should be done in covert operations.

But either the people moved too fast or his senses had not recovered sufficiently to act on his rage. By the time his vision cleared, the gaps in the crowd were too large. There were too

many lights, cops, hawkers, and peddlers, and too much traffic to dodge through. So he retreated to the subway and, dar-
ing anyone to step on his toe, made his way back uptown.

"Be all you can be." Har, har . . .

It rang in his ears, invaded his senses, took control of his
will so that when he blinked, he found himself back on Strivers' Row again, standing across the street from Gray Eyes'
house. The last remnants of daylight had faded and night
spread like a thick cloak. A few pedestrians strolled by, none
glancing his way, but he watched them, feeling safe hidden in
the shadow of the trees. When their footsteps faded, he was
left alone again with his thoughts.

Lights on. Wonder what she up to. Wonder if she—

He heard more footsteps and glanced in the direction of
Frederick Douglass Boulevard. His eyes widened as if he
couldn't believe what he saw.

*Shit! It's her. Walkin' right there. Ain't this a bitch. She right
there . . .*

The sight of her, walking alone, stunned him, left him no
time to revel in the feeling that welled up in him before he
heard something else.

*You got to move on this one, Ache. Fast. Step on across. Head
her off. Once she reach that door, she home free. You don't want
that. Head the bitch off. Now. This. Is. It.*

He edged between the parked cars and sidled across the
street, tipping on the balls of his feet. Now he looked neither
left nor right, up nor down the block, but kept her fastened in

the crosshairs of his narrowed vision. A small gust of wind eddied up, filling his nostrils with the smell of his sweat. Water gathered in the hollow of his back, and his shirt stuck to him. She was less than three feet away, moving slowly. Her head was down, as if she was looking for something she might have dropped on the ground. An earring, maybe.

His hand closed on the razor so tightly that pinpricks of pain cramped his fingers. The noise in his head grew, crowding out everything. All he saw was her.

Comin' right at me. Right at me.

He gazed at the striped T-shirt and black shorts.

Just ease the blade out, squeeze it to my side till she get juuuusst . . .

"Mali! Say!"

He saw her look up, whirl toward the sound as the car door opened. An older man stepped out of a Lincoln Town Car and said to the driver, "Hold on, buddy. Be back in a second," then turned to her. "This is what happens when I rush out. I forgot my—"

The rest was lost in the storm that swelled in Ache's head. Now the oak door opened and the dog, barking, bounded down the steps, its paws clacking hard on the pavement. It skidded to a halt so near him he could feel its moist breath. Then he heard a voice, her voice, float through a foggy ether.

"Come on, Ruffin. Back in the house now, boy. Come on." The dog trotted to her side. She patted his thick neck, then, holding his collar, they passed so close he caught the faint scent of her perfume above the stink of his sweat. The razor was in his hand, and his hand was like a block of ice at his side.

He pivoted in a half-circle, stumbling as if he had been sideswiped by a slow-moving car. At the corner of Frederick Douglass, when he was able to swallow, the blood backed up in his throat and he knew that the inside of his mouth had been sucked in and bitten raw. Later, when he was able to free his hand, the razor slipped back in his pocket, but it was some time before he managed to find his way home.

Two weeks ago. But he still saw the gray eyes, still heard Hazel's dry laugh. "Be all you can be."

Now he turned over on the bed and listened to the noise drifting from the living room. Jerry had probably said something profound and Hazel was agreeing with him. He turned off the fifteen-watt light and fanned his fingers along the dusty floor under the bed.

Blade still there, Ache. Just chill. You'll get her. Thing is not to get caught.

chapter

twenty-five

I folded my arms on the dining table and waited, feeling my patience ebbing away by the second. The day had dawned so beautifully, with a crisp breeze waking me, pulling me out of a bed I'd spent too much time in. I had taken a trial run last night and Dad had nearly gone through the roof when he stepped out of that cab. But the short walk convinced me that I was ready to do some serious stepping: pound the pavement, rejoin the ranks of the living, breathing, walking, singing, fighting, ordinary folks. I hit a hurdle before the breakfast dishes were even cleared.

Dad was on his second cup of coffee, taking his time, as if he had not even heard me.

"It's not like I'm going out to run a marathon," I repeated. "I'm only walking a few blocks. The swelling's practically gone and I can get my sneaker on without complaining."

He didn't bother to look up from his newspaper but I heard a low grumph as he turned a page. I leaned nearer, clasping my hands as if awaiting a papal blessing.

Finally he said, "At least let Alvin walk with you. I'll take Ruffin out later. You shouldn't try to handle him just yet."

I sighed and thought of genuflecting in gratitude but decided it was simpler to say: "Don't worry about me, Dad. I'll be all right."

Once outside, I made it down the four steps easily and felt the pavement again beneath my feet. I wanted to shout but contained myself as Alvin and I walked toward Powell Boulevard.

Alvin, after some intensive sessions with Dr. Thomas, who lived two doors away, had recovered from the nightmare of James's death and was able to talk about it freely.

He did not mention it now but was interested in how far I was able to walk. "Can you make it to the ball court?"

"I guess so. Your crew on today?"

"Naw, just a pickup game, but Clarence has somebody who wants to talk to you."

"What about? Who is it?"

"Guy named Yo-Yo. Something he saw a while back. Clarence didn't have time to mention it before because all this other stuff came down—about James and all—and I guess we all just forgot."

I nodded and we walked slowly, Alvin absorbed in Erykah Badu pumping the promise of young love from his CD Walkman, and I taking in everything the avenue had to offer and trying to figure out what I'd missed.

The long-haulers were still parked near the old Renaissance Ballroom, their tables overflowing with southern produce. The windows of Smalls Paradise were still sealed. Street vendors still sailed by with their portable inventories displayed in supermarket shopping carts, or sample cases suspended from the neck to be snapped shut in case of rain or cops.

The more imaginative peddlers draped the stuff over their arms and around their necks, allowing a dozen or so scarves, ties, and belts to flow in the wind.

At every other corner, curbside barbecue cookers scented the air. Two tour buses rumbled to a stop at 132nd Street and discharged a group that crowded into Wells Restaurant, chattering and working their Leicas and ready for the chicken and waffles.

At 127th Street Clarence was alone on the court, dribbling the ball in a dizzy display under the basket, then leaping in a fast tight semicircle to sink it. I watched his lean form cut the air like a gazelle and understood how impressed the college recruiter must have been.

Clarence was also an excellent singer, so he managed to win two scholarships. Alvin had met him as a member of the Uptown Children's Chorus where Clarence's bass voice practically shook the walls of the rehearsal room. He had nicknamed Alvin "Striver" when he found out he lived on Strivers' Row and Alvin had nicknamed him "main man" after he had gotten me out of a bad jam a few years ago.

Clarence's mother, young, attractive, and severely abused by a former boyfriend, was still struggling with drug addiction, so Morris's mother, Mrs. Johnson, provided Clarence with meals and a safe zone when his mom's life tumbled into periodic chaos. My dad had gotten him a part-time maintenance job at the club, and during the school year I tutored him twice a week.

He expected to graduate next spring and attend Savannah State College on the scholarships and I'd already contacted my friend, a nursing supervisor who lived in Savannah. I could count on her sharp eye and tough love to keep him on the straight and narrow while he was there.

Alvin and I sat on the bench near the water fountain and watched Clarence sail through a dozen layups, clearing the rim each time. Finally he stopped and headed toward us, holding the ball in the crook of his arm, his dark skin glistening from the exercise.

"Hey, Striver. What's goin' on? Miss Mali, I see your leg is better. You walkin' all right. That's nice. That's nice."

"Thanks, it's coming along," I said. "Alvin said you had someone who wanted to talk to me."

"Yeah, he might have something you can use. Striver thought you might be here today so I got word out. Yo-Yo show any minute now."

I wondered where the name came from and Clarence, who seemed able to read minds like most teenagers I knew, said, "Real name's Tommy Walker but he do the deaf thing sometime when we callin' him. Like we gotta go, 'Yo. Yo!' two times before he turn around and it sorta stuck, you know what I'm sayin'?"

That last phrase ran together so that it came out "nom-sane?"

"Did he say why he wanted to speak to me?"

"Well, I kinda suggested it. He don't really know you but he said he wanted to maybe exchange some information. And it hadda be with somebody he could trust. It went down like this, Miss Mali. I'm in the park one night bouncin' a few balls, the only one out here, and he come easin' 'round the way, through those trees, nearly scared me out my shoes. I ask him what was happenin' and he say he was jammed. He'll tell you when he show."

Clarence had sat down next to me on the bench and rolled the ball in a small circle with his foot. I saw that with the small salary he'd earned, he was finally able to trade in his worn-out sneakers with the shredded laces for a new pair. To his credit, he had passed up the $150 hype and opted for a less expensive model.

"Where does Yo-Yo live?"

"In that big house on Seventh near 130th Street. I don't know the number but it's on the west side of the avenue, right next door to that store used to be a picture framin' shop."

I closed my eyes and tried to picture the house.

Morris showed up and ten minutes later another young man entered the park. He stepped cautiously as Clarence approached him. He whispered something and Clarence pointed to me, then brought him over.

"This is Yo—I mean Tommy Walker," and he left us alone and joined Alvin and Morris at the far end of the court.

Yo-Yo shook my hand and sat down like an old man who'd just conquered a hard flight of stairs. His hello was hesitant and he avoided my gaze. I knew then that Clarence had already told him of my connection—or former connection—with the NYPD and he needed to know if I could be trusted. I waited in silence, giving him time to make up his mind.

Finally I said, "Clarence said you wanted to talk to me."

I glanced at him as he watched Alvin and Morris and Clarence and I was unsure if he was concentrating on the ball or on an answer that wouldn't reveal too much. When he finally started to speak, his voice was low but he got to the point quickly.

"Miss Mali. The thing I'm lookin' for is a guarantee that I won't have to do state time. Hard time."

"What happened?"

"Violated parole. There's a warrant out. I'm lookin' at state time."

His gaze veered away from me and he squinted at Alvin, Morris, and Clarence making their moves in center court. He followed the action but the veins on the side of his neck stood out like knotted cable.

"Listen," I said, "I don't want to know why or how you violated parole. But you did say there's a warrant out. Clarence said you wanted to speak to someone you could trust, maybe cut a deal. What've you got that I can use?"

When he spoke, I listened, nodded appropriately, and remained quiet. I did not want, under any circumstance, to scare this young man away. A minute later he stopped and looked around.

"Listen, can we go someplace else? Maybe a little more private?"

I looked around also. No point in having the warrant squad swoop down before I got the full story. "Whatever you say."

I glanced at my watch, then waved down the court at Alvin, Morris, and Clarence. "See you guys later."

"Yo, Mali. Where you heading?" Alvin dropped the ball and came running, a frown creasing his face.

"Bob's Restaurant," I said. "I'll be okay."

He looked doubtful. "You take it slow, you hear me?"

I nodded, wondering if he'd been hanging with Dad so long he'd absorbed his speeches, line by line, along with his tendency to worry.

He stared hard at Tommy as if to memorize some particular mark or mole in case I was kidnapped and he'd have to track him to Alaska or something.

"Be seein' you, Yo-Yo."

Tommy nodded, seeming to understand. "Everything's cool."

We left the park and headed downtown. He strolled beside me silently, for three blocks, carefully scrutinizing any car that slowed and any beat cop who looked our way. Tommy was young—twenty years old at most—and not as tall as I. He was muscular and walked on the tips of his sneakers, bouncing forward like a boxer in training. His T-shirt read "Million Man March" and I wondered if he had attended.

At the door of a small restaurant that I thought was private enough, he hesitated.

"What if you can't use what I got to say? What if . . . ?"

I touched his shoulder and opened the door. "What I've heard so far is very interesting. I want to hear the rest."

chapter

twenty-six

Bob's Restaurant, just off Seventh Avenue and 122nd Street, was so small that almost everyone agreed it was better to take out a dinner than eat at one of the four postage-sized booths that crowded the place. But the food was so good the crowd never stopped coming.

Despite the afternoon heat, the dim lighting and the exotic ferns that decorated the window made the place seem cool inside. The overhead fan rotated the air rising from the kitchen and sent it back down again, not cool but rich with the aroma of simmering oxtails, baked chicken, cheese baked macaroni, collard greens, cabbage sautéed in garlic butter, and candied yams.

Behind the narrow counter, Bob, an implausibly slim, middle-aged man who was the cook, waiter, and owner, moved back and forth among the pots and pans. A sign above the narrow counter read:

Yes, I Eat My Own Cooking
but God Blessed Me with Skinny Genes
So Don't Ask. Just Enjoy.

"Be with y'all in a minute," he said. "Grab a seat." He waved toward the one available booth and I watched his toque disappear among the forest of overhanging copper-bottomed pans in the kitchen.

We sat in a high-back booth facing the kitchen. It was situated away from the window and Tommy preferred to sit facing the door. Bob had turned on the radio and WBGO jazz masked the nearby conversation, but Tommy still kept his voice low as he leaned forward and folded his arms on the Formica table.

"I didn't get jammed on nuthin' real bad. Not like no gun charge or nuthin', you know. Just dumb shit. Cursed out my P.O. down at his office and didn't show up again when I was supposed to. I don't know why I did that. I mean, the brother was okay. He was cool, you know. Didn't treat me like some a them white cowboys, come bustin' in your door with they hand on they gun, one foot on the floor and the other ready to go up your ass. With the brother, it was always Mr. Walker this and Mr. Walker that. Respect, you know what I'm sayin'?

"But I was dealin' with some heavy personal pressure at the time. My aunt was on my case, wantin' me to get a gig, 'cause you know every parolee supposed to have a job. But how you supposed to get one if you ain't trained to do nuthin'? Well anyway, I know it's too late for excuses. I fucked up and hard time is starin' me in the face."

"Not necessarily . . ."

When Bob in his waiter's role came to the table, Tommy was nervous and settled for iced tea, no sugar. I examined the menu, skipped the heavy stuff, and went for the peach cobbler with two scoops of butter pecan ice cream and whipped-cream topping. Enough to hold me through this meeting.

We remained silent until Bob moved back away, then I said, "Sounds like you're having a tough time, no job and all . . ."

He eased his hands across the table, peeled off a napkin from the dispenser, and twisted it around his fingers as he spoke.

". . . okay, here's what I got. I was on my roof one night about three weeks ago. Too damn hot. Room felt like a oven. I know I got curfew but least I wasn't hangin' at the corner. Technically I was home, you know what I'm sayin'? Technically. And I was on the roof—"

"Alone?" I asked, even though he'd said so earlier.

"Aah, yeah. Solo."

"What were you doing?"

"Well, I—"

He hesitated again and I saw the sweat stand out on his clean-shaven head, form a thin rivulet, and arc at his thick eyebrows. He had high North Carolina Cherokee cheekbones and deep-set eyes that telegraphed his fear of returning to prison. As tough as he seemed, he was also quite handsome, and returning to prison meant having to fight not only for his manhood but possibly for his life.

He had been living with his aunt on the top floor of a five-story walkup on Powell Boulevard since his release six months ago and needed to talk someplace away from home because his aunt would evict him if she found out he'd messed up again.

"Look," I said, "forget about what you were doing. What did you see?"

I reached into the dispenser and handed him another napkin and waited as he wiped his face.

"Well, I ain't too sure what I seen. I mean it was dark and all, you know. Midnight, I think."

He glanced at me and added, "Or maybe it was a little earlier, I ain't too sure. Anyway, I'm there and the dude come up on me swift, you know. I thought it was the Five-O at first and I, like, froze. Homeboy so swift he didn't even see me. But I saw him though. Got a deep peep. He was wide-eyed, grinnin' like a fuckin' Halloween pumpkin. Eyes all wide and shit. Like he was high on somethin'. And he was talkin' to himself, mumblin' . . .''

"What was he saying?" I asked, looking up from a napkin I'd started to scribble on.

Tommy shrugged and spread his hands out on the table. His fingers were long and thin, but I noticed the slight tremor.

"I couldn't catch it 'cause he was mumblin', crazylike, and he was walkin' funny. Wide-legged. Like he had just . . .'' He glanced at me again and hesitated, then decided that, having been on the force, I'd probably heard it all before.

"He, ah, look like he had just come on himself," he whispered, avoiding my gaze. "And his underwear mighta been sticky or somethin'. I don't know. Homie was too strange is all I can say.''

He wiped the bridge of his nose again, closed his eyes, and pressed the napkin to his forehead.

"What did he look like?"

"Lessee. Dark skin. Average build. Real big arms. 'Bout my height, I guess, but I can't be too sure 'cause I was on the—you know, that curve of the roof that slants up to the edge? Well, like soon as I heard the roof door bang open, I rolled right into the curve. Hell, wasn't no place to run. If it was the Five-O, I wasn't takin' no bullet in the back just so some blueshirt could git a promotion on me. Uhn-uhn. I laid right in the cut, figurin' they'd take a pass. When I ain't seen no flashlight pop, I knew it wasn't the real thing, but I laid anyway, and watched this crazy motherfucka and wondered what was gonna go down next. Come to think of it, I could even smell 'im. Boy funkier than government cheese.''

''What was he wearing?''

''Some kinda dark pants. Maybe the kind you go joggin' in, I think. Sneakers. Dark T-shirt with some writin' on the back but I ain't too sure about that neither. I mean I couldn't read it bein' that it was dark. And I can't tell you what his face look like normal 'cause, like I said, it was all twisted up and he had a grin you ain't gonna see 'cept maybe on fright night. I wanna know what kinda bomb shit he was on, man.''

He glanced at me again and added quickly, ''So I could stay away from it, you know what I mean. He scared me so bad, like if I *hadda* been high, I woulda crashed in a flash.''

''Was he carrying anything?''

''Come to think of it, some kinda package, small. Fit under his arm. Couldna been nothin' heavy 'cause it didn't slow 'im down none. Also, his hands looked white, shiny . . .''

I folded the napkin. Tommy pushed the glass, empty now except for the ice, to the middle of the table and looked at me expectantly. ''I live in the same building where that lady was murdered. The same building, you know what I'm sayin' . . .''

I sat in the silence watching the faint trace of ice cream melt over the crumbs of my peach cobbler and watching Tommy twist the paper napkin to shreds.

Tommy lived in the same building Marie had lived in.

There had been cornflakes scattered on her body but no box had been recovered. The killer had taken it. And there were no prints anywhere on the scene.

"I want you to speak to someone," I whispered. "A Detective Honeywell. He should be able to work something out with your P.O."

chapter

twenty-seven

The temperature was hovering near ninety when I left the restaurant and the pavement radiated enough heat to penetrate the soles of my sneakers. Powell Boulevard at 3:00 P.M. was practically deserted except for the speeding traffic and a few somnolent pedestrians who seemed too dazed to figure out that they shouldn't be outdoors in the first place, except in an emergency.

The minute I stepped in the house, I turned the air up full-force and ran a bath of lukewarm water scented with hibiscus. A half hour later my head was clear enough to again pore over my notebook and transfer the notes from my conversation with Yo-Yo. I settled in the chair by the window with a pitcher of iced tea and read the earlier entries. I had drawn a diagram—two overlapping circles which I'd labeled "Bronx" and "Harlem." Three lines, like wheel spokes, radiated from each circle and held the names of the women. In the small space common to both circles, I had scribbled the word "cornflakes."

Below the circles were lines of description.

The Bronx women, according to Tad's Four-Eight source, were single, lived alone, and had no children. All had well-paying jobs or professions, yet nothing had been stolen from the apartments. One of the Bronx women, a young Latina, had worked as a bank loan officer; the second, a thirty-year-old African American, had been a general office manager for a fashion house; and the third, an African American, about thirty-eight, had been a supervising service representative for a cable television company.

Below the "Harlem" circle, I noted that Claudine had been a teacher, Marie a postal clerk, and Felicia an artist.

I kept going back to the space where the circles overlapped, and what Yo-Yo had said: "some kinda package, small. Fit under his arm. Couldna been nothin' heavy 'cause it didn't slow 'im down none. Also, his hands looked white, shiny . . ."

What was the man carrying? An empty box? Was he wearing gloves, latex gloves, white and shiny?

I scanned my earlier notes: the likely places he could have watched the women, studied them until he had their routine together. Like jazz clubs, restaurants, gyms, post offices, banks, museums, galleries, schools. I crossed these out and folded my arms on the windowsill, listening to the murmur of the songbirds outside. They sounded muted, as if they were being parboiled by the rolling power of the sun.

I finished the iced tea, got dressed again, and left the cool comfort of the house. By the time I strolled the few blocks to Bertha's beauty salon, the temperature had taken its toll again and I was glad to see the inside of her shop despite the high-decibel soap opera blasting from the television.

When I stepped in, she lowered the volume, but not by much. Her face, wreathed in a short feathered auburn cut, lit up when she saw me.

"Girl, you on the move again, thank God. Seein' you laid up in the hospital scared the hell outta me. Thought I was about to lose my friend."

"I guess it wasn't my time," I said, settling into one of the two chairs. A tall gangly girl of about eleven or twelve with a crown of tight curly ringlets had just vacated the other chair and stared at my two-inch 'fro, clearly wondering what miracle Bertha was going to perform for me, but I had no wish to explain. She would not have understood what Bert's twenty-year friendship meant, nor the therapeutic benefits of the scalp massages that I indulged in from time to time.

Bertha counted out the change, the girl murmured a polite thank-you and glanced at me again before stepping out into the afternoon heat.

Bertha moved to place a handful of combs into the sterilizer. "So, girl, how you doin'?"

I did not answer but continued to gaze out of the window at the deserted avenue thinking of Yo-Yo and of the overlapping circles in my notebook. Finally I picked up the newspaper lying near the dryer and scanned the ads. The food section contained the usual diet advice, cooking advice, menus, and grocery coupons. I also scanned the flyer distributed by the supermarket.

"You mighty quiet, Mali. Prices can't be that bad. Thin as you are, you probably don't eat that much anyway."

When I didn't respond, she said, "You all right?"

"I'm all right. I was just wondering—when do you shop for groceries?"

She gave me a look that said, "Car accident did something to my girl's brain. She jumpin' from one thing to another."

"Usually on Wednesdays," she said, still looking at me, probably searching for additional signs of dementia. "I go when the sales are advertised, or the day after. That store got pretty good prices.

"One time I had my stuff delivered but I decided that's for folks too busy to be pullin' a shoppin' cart back and forth. Me, I don't mind doin' it. I figure if I sweat a few pounds luggin' that pint of butter pecan, it kinda balance things out when I dip into it 'round midnight.

"Beside, the one time I had my stuff delivered, boy was so ugly—"

"Did he look ugly or did he act ugly?" I said, glancing from the flyer and sitting up in the chair.

"Both."

"What did he do?"

Bertha had reached into a large plastic bag, pulled out an armload of white towels, and begun to fold and stack them on the narrow counter. She stopped now and gazed toward the window in concentration.

"Well, that's a funny question 'cause you know, he really didn't do anything but I kinda felt something. He stepped in, put the bags down—rather, he slammed 'em down—and had this look—like a dog has when the world is kickin' 'im in the behind. Boy didn't crack a smile when I said it was a good thing he wasn't deliverin' eggs.

"He was mad at somethin' or somebody so I didn't let 'im take one step further into this place. Don't need no bad vibes floatin' 'round when I'm tryin' to hit a number. And you know how the Five-O or the FBI can tag somebody by their DNA thing? Well, I work my own test. I looked at him and I said to myself, 'Mmhmm. DNA *Dat Negro Anxious.*' So I give 'im a tip and had him tip right on out. Then I locked my door."

"You locked your door?" I said. "You never do that."

Bert stopped folding again and held up her hand. "Well, there's a first time for everything. I know he ain't darkened my doorway again. I walk to that store, do my own shoppin' and deliver my own stuff, and I'm satisfied. Besides, who knows what these delivery guys be pilferin', then turn around and sell the stuff on the street, sometimes right back to the person they stole it from. Hell with that. I ain't got time to be checkin' every bottle, bag, and box. If I bring it home, I know it's there."

I stared out of the window, listening as she spoke. . . . *Don't have time to check every item I buy. Probably sell it back to the person they stole it from.*

Or perhaps bring it back. Bring it back. Is this what he did?

"What did he look like?"

Bert touched her hand to her chin again. "Ah, lessee. Damn, that was a while ago and you know my brain ain't functionin' too tough in this heat. But I kinda remember him bein' about maybe twenty-two or twenty-three years old, me-dium height, dark brown complexion, hair cut close, and had real big arms—like he was into weights or somethin'."

"You eat cereal? Cornflakes?"

She looked at me again and I could practically hear the wheels turning, wondering what was coming, but she only shook her head. "Girl, you ask the damnedest things. But no. I'm a grits and greens girl from way back. No cereal for me." Then she leaned over and scanned the flyer. "Why? You got a coupon or somethin'? I'm big on coupons."

"No," I answered. "No coupon. Just an idea."

When I left the shop, a mass of thunderclouds had moved in, blotting out the sun and easing the temperature down a few degrees. More folks were in the street now, and moving fast, intent on completing as many errands as possible before the storm broke. I didn't hurry because my next stop was only three blocks away.

On 136th Street between Frederick Douglass Boulevard and Edgecombe Avenue, I stopped in front of Felicia Temple's brownstone where a For Sale sign had been tacked above the door.

I rang the bell and waited a few seconds, not sure if anyone was in the house. I was heading back down the steps when I heard the lock turn behind me.

"May I help you?"

A short, round, middle-aged woman stared down the steps at me. She seemed determined to smile through some profound anguish. "Are you here to see the house?"

"Well, yes," I said, making my way back to the door. We stepped inside and the woman said, "I'm Irene, the housekeeper. I'll be here until the place is sold. If you have any questions . . ."

She whispered but her echo carried through the room and she walked softly as if we were treading on sacred ground. I glanced at her sad expression and decided to tell the truth.

"I'm Mali Anderson," I said.

"Mali Anderson? Were you here before?"

"No. I'm Jeffrey Anderson's daughter. My dad was a friend of Ms. Temple."

She put her hand to her mouth and smiled. "Oh. Oh, yes. Your father and Ms. Temple were very good friends. I—oh, this is so . . ." She paused, searching for the words in the silence. "You have an idea how I'm feeling about this situation. I've worked for Ms. Temple for so long, I can't believe she's . . ." The small smile faded as she retrieved a tissue from her pocket.

"I'm supposed to keep an eye on things until everything is settled, but sometimes, at night, I listen, and I feel like she's moving around right near me. I'm not afraid or anything but I can't tell you how much I miss her. Maybe so much so that I'm imagining things. Sometimes I think I can still hear her laughter."

I nodded. "My dad said the same thing. How she laughed, smiled, seemed to light up every place she entered. He enjoyed being in her company."

We walked through the double parlor and stood for a minute in the back room. The rooms were large but seemed vast in their emptiness. I glanced at the pink-marbled fireplaces, the pier mirrors, the intricate moldings adorning the ceiling. Sunlight splashed through the Tiffany glass windows in the rear and imprinted a pattern of red, yellow, and blue on the parquet floor. Irene, still holding the tissue, gazed out into the garden.

"This is where she did most of her work. Right down there." Then she turned to appraise me with her sad eyes.

"I suppose your dad . . . How did he take it? I know it's been a while, but is he all right?"

"My father," I said without exaggeration, "was deeply affected. He misses her very much."

She turned from the window and we made our way slowly back toward the front of the house. "I simply don't know how it happened," she whispered. "I turn my back for one minute and she's gone. Somehow I can't help feeling that if I'd only been here. If I'd only—but no, I decided to go to Florida to help my sister organize my niece's wedding. Something they could've done themselves. They didn't need me. I see now that I was probably intruding on something they could've handled very well without me. I could've simply gone as a guest and returned the next day. But no. I had to go and leave Ms. Temple here to fend for herself."

She looked at me quickly and smiled a weak smile. Her dark, round face was lined around the mouth and her eyelids were crinkled from days and nights of crying.

"No, I didn't mean that 'fend for herself' thing. My God, she was a grown woman, perfectly able to care for herself, but she was too busy to do certain things, you know what I mean. Cleaning and ironing and cooking and shopping. I came here every day and that's what I did. She had her job and I had mine."

"This is a big place. Housekeeping must've kept you very busy."

"Oh, I enjoyed it, especially the cooking. And the shopping was no problem. Supermarket right there on Lenox. Everything delivered fresh. Every Wednesday. Sometimes when she wanted something special, I'd take the bus down to the

Union Square green market, but usually I shopped on Lenox, because it was so convenient."

"I suppose you'll be sorry when the house is sold . . ."

"Sorry, yes. But sort of glad too. I can't tell you how upsetting this whole thing has been. Discovering her in that horrible, horrible condition. With all that—"

"With all that what?" I whispered when it seemed that she wasn't going to go on.

When she was able to continue, she nodded quickly, as if to shake the image. "She didn't even eat cereal," she murmured, more to herself than to me. "The cereal was for me. And the police asking all those questions I couldn't answer."

"Like what?" I said, not wanting to follow up on the cereal question. I had enough information already.

"Well, like did anyone have a grudge against her? Did she owe anyone money? Did she have any enemies? Had she received any strange phone calls? Things I knew nothing about. Then they wanted a list of my relatives, especially the male relatives. Wanted to know if I had left my keys with any of them. On top of my loss, I had to listen to that. I was so upset I went to bed and couldn't get up for days. My doctor had to give me medicine to calm my nerves."

She looked at me and snapped her fingers. "Ah, here I am, going on and on. Painting such a bad picture. At this rate, the house will never get sold. You're not interested in the place, are you?"

"No, but my dad spoke of her so often I wanted to see the house before it was sold. It's magnificent."

"You should've seen it when it was furnished," she sighed.

The bell rang again and Irene looked at her watch. "Expecting a young couple, doctor and his wife. Wife's a painter, just like Ms. Temple was. They've been here twice already and I think they're leaning toward . . ."

She walked to the door, her footsteps sounding hollow across the empty room. I followed, knowing that my visit was over.

chapter

twenty-eight

Ache leaned out of the bedroom window and took another draw from his dwindling stash. The blunt was so hot it burned his fingertips. The clock across the street above the drugstore read nearly 10:00 P.M., time for Hazel's talk shows to wind down. He waited patiently, holding the acrid smoke in his lungs as long as he could without choking, feeling no anger, no fear, just extra good. Even the voice that he usually listened to was quiet except to let him know that whatever was gonna go down would just have to go down, that's all. This was it.

He'd reached this point several times before, smoked half a bag once, only to have his courage drain away when he moved down the hall and approached the living room. Now he extinguished the smoke, dragging the reefer-filled cigar along the window ledge, and watched the tiny sparks waft like fireflies into the night. When they disappeared completely, he turned from the window to face his darkened room.

This is different.

He heard his footsteps moving. They sounded loud enough to drown out Hazel's laughter as she clicked the remote, surfing the channels. The paper in his hand felt damp from his sweat but he didn't care.

This is different.

Hazel looked up from the sofa and her smile disappeared at the sight of him. "What's eatin' you? I don't wanna hear no shit about you bein' mugged again."

"It ain't that. It's this," he answered, surprised that his voice was so steady. "It's this," he repeated, liking the way he sounded.

Hazel peered at the piece of paper in front of her and jerked back as if a snake had slithered across her lap.

"Where the fuck you get that? You been riflin' in my things?"

"I needed it to show the recruitment people. They wouldn't let me take the test without it." He heard his voice waver and he grew angry as he felt his resolve begin to disintegrate under her stare.

"So what good did it do you? No GED, you couldn't even get in the door."

He held the paper so tightly it was in danger of shredding. "Yeah. I know. It says here that Nathan Milton is—"

"I know what the fuck it says. I put it there, didn't I?"

"Well, I—"

"Well you nuthin'! You wanna know why it's on there? You wanna know what happened? I'll tell you about that son of a bitch, Nathan Milton. I'll tell you what he did."

She rose from the sofa abruptly, and instead of moving toward him, he was surprised to see her edge away, staring at him as if he had mutated into some alien thing. She maneuvered until she could go no further and leaned against the wall.

"Our daddy," she said. Her voice sounded as if she had swallowed marbles. He listened, dumbfounded, as she went on. "Yours and mine. You didn't know that, did you? No, you too dumb to know anything. But you shoulda known somethin' was up. You got the same damn ugly face. Every time I see you, I see him. He the one. Goddamn sommabitch.

"I'm fifteen," she said, raising her hand to her chest. "Fifteen, and he come in the midnight hour, all fortied up, tellin' me I oughtta be glad. Ugly and fat as I am, nobody want me anyway so be glad he willin' to do the job.

"That's what he said and that's what he did, climbed on

and started workin' me, all the while calling me fat. Ugly. My own daddy. Your daddy. But after the third time, when I knew his shit was gonna be a habit, I sat down and figured out everything. I may be fat and I may be ugly but I got a brain. I figured out that rat bait work on the biggest rat. All you got to do is mix enough of it with sugar and put it in the coffee."

She did not pause to see what effect this had on her son but moved away from the wall and toward the television, the remote gripped in her fist like a weapon.

"Even the fuckin' doctors couldn't tell or didn't wanna be bothered tellin'. They didn't cut 'im open or nuthin'. Looked at that gut blown up like a balloon and said it was 'pendicitis. That was the first time in my whole life I got to smile. Imagine that. 'Pendicitis. Ain't that a laugh.

"He gone but you still here. You still here. And every time I look at you, I hear how ugly I am. You don't even have to open your mouth and I hear him. It's like a radio ain't never been turned off."

They faced each other, squared off like boxers in a ring too small to maneuver in, too confined to avoid the blows.

"So now you know, and can't do nuthin' about it. Can't do shit! He already checked out, and I"—she slapped her hand to her chest proudly—"I did it. Me! I beat you to it!"

He did not move from the doorway but stared at her as she walked back toward the sagging couch. He had not seen her take this many steps in years, and when she moved, the folds shook under the filthy, tentlike dress.

He tried to imagine her at fifteen and wondered what had

changed except that she'd given birth to someone who never should have been born.

Rat bait. His emotions seesawed between admiration—a keen, unfamiliar sensation—for her using the poison and profound hatred for how she'd made him pay. Day after day after day.

And he thought of the one earlier instance when she'd moved this fast. That time, when he had given up, when he stood on the counter so hungry he trembled, and jimmied the lock on the cabinet. Food was behind the lock and he hadn't seen any the entire day. He had listened to her snores and tried to work fast, absorbed in the thought of what he would find. He knew it was food. It had to be food, because she kept it locked up tight.

The cabinet opened under the light pressure of the butter knife and a whole store was stacked before him, more than he'd seen at one time in one place in all his eight years.

He'd reached for the nearest and largest item, a box of corn-flakes, and stepped from the counter onto the stool but it collapsed under his shaking weight, sending him to the floor to stare in fright at the scattered cereal and then at his mother standing in the doorway.

He was surprised at how quietly she worked, sweeping it up slowly. Then she looked around thoughtfully and began to sweep under the table, in the corners, angled the broom into the narrow greasy space between the stove and the fridge, pulling out the dirt, dustballs, cobwebs, dead roaches, roach shells, roach eggs, and quietly mixed it all in with the cereal.

Then in one swift maneuver, caught him in a choke hold and slammed him and the box of cereal into the hall closet.

He'd had no idea how long he was inside because there was no light. All he knew was that he ate the cereal, swallowed the dirt, consumed the roaches, vomited on himself, and then ate some more. He kept eating, trying to fill the hole in his stomach which seemed to grow larger with each fistful he brought to his mouth.

The box was empty when the key turned again and one of her "overnighters"—the old nice West Indian one who, when he spoke fast, could hardly be understood—lifted him out, stripped his soiled clothes, and rushed him into the bathtub.

"God damn, Hazel! When you gon' stop treat de boy like a yard dog? Smell like fuckin' shithouse for sure."

And she had yelled, "You want 'im, Pop?"

That was the first time in a month that he'd touched water, actually bathed, and while he strained to scour away the filth, he strained to listen. He heard her laughter roll down the hall like a cascade of stones.

"I'm axin' you, Pop. Do you want 'im?"

"Awh, mind now, girl. God watchin' you, you know . . ."

He remained still, trying not to splash, waiting for the response from the old man that might have delivered him, but it never came.

He heard low murmurs and an occasional giggle as they popped the cans of beer and whispered some more and he waited and waited until the water had grown cold but they had forgotten about him.

He watched her settle back on the sofa, her chest heaving as if she had run a mile.

"So what you gonna do now that you know? What difference it make to you?"

None at all, he wanted to say, but he could not answer. He moved away and allowed the scrap of paper, stained with his sweat, to fall to the floor.

See, Ache. I coulda told you what the deal was. I knew it was somethin' funny went down, but you know . . . looka here. Here's what you gotta do . . .

In the room, he lay down on the bed and squeezed his eyes tight, trying to shut out the sounds that seemed to flow out from the cracks in the peeling paint.

Whatcha gonna do . . . Friday comin'. You ain't got two coins to rub together. Not even for a hot dog. Can't sneak in that kitchen. End up in that closet again. No food. No money. She kick you to the curb and you be nuthin'. She told you you was nuthin'.

He opened his eyes wide now, staring into the dark, straining as the images came into focus. Ragged Natalie, the little girl left on the roof with the smile frozen on her face; the silver-haired artist in the garden who'd looked right through him; the pretty woman on Edgecombe who'd invited him in for that glass of water; the tough-talking sister on Seventh Avenue who'd put up one hell of a fight. And there were those three in the Bronx, anonymous and innocent.

He saw them all, and remembered how the smiles had iced over when they realized, too late, what was happening. He saw them and the deep warm feeling welled up like a spring.

They knew I was somethin'. Knew I didn't take no shit.

Then the image of Mercy Anne drifted from the shadows, her eyes like silver discs. She opened her mouth and the laughter made him sit up. Or was it Hazel down the hall? The television was on again and the laughter flowed toward him.

He thought of the Gray Eyes who came in for that ice cream and made him lose his job, and thought of how he'd nearly connected the other night if only that cab and that damn dog . . .

Bile exploded in the back of his throat and he was off the sagging mattress, down on his knees, rummaging under the bed. His stash—what was left of it—was safe because Hazel could never kneel down in a million years to search the space.

His fingers sifted through the dust until he felt the coil of wire and the box of gloves but he reached past this until his fingers closed on the razor.

He could see the house again, sheltered beneath the thick-leafed trees lining the curb like sentries. Strivers' Row. Gray Eyes was living large while he had no job, no money. He closed his eyes again, visualizing the door to her house. A door of intricately carved oak.

Hell, it ain't gonna be like last time. All you do is ring the bell and she open the door. Hazel worked her rat stuff . . . fooled all them motherfuckers. Every one of 'em. You smart just like her. All that shit you perpetrated and ain't got busted yet. That tell you somethin' right there. Tell you, you way better than her any day. All you got to do is walk to that door.

chapter

twenty-nine

I tacked the sketches on the wall above my desk and stepped
back to gaze at them from different angles. Based on the description Yo-Yo had given the artist at the precinct, I wondered if he had been smoking something special that night on
the roof, when I showed the drawing to Bertha, she had
stepped back as if she'd been hit. "Damn! Where you dig that
up from?"

This poster brother had a face that would force a plastic
surgeon into retirement. The eyes resembled a frog who'd

been surprised by a larger predator and his mouth was stretched wide enough to swallow a plate. His face was clean-shaven but his hairline ended in a widow's peak a few inches above his eyebrows.

The other drawing based on Ms. Irene's description wasn't much better, but neither Bertha nor Miss Irene would confirm positively that the drawing was that of the man who had delivered their groceries. Bertha had looked at it and then shook her head.

"I don't know, Mali. I just don't know for sure. I mean the brother was ugly and nervous, but that don't mean he's a criminal. I'd hate to finger the wrong man. Remember how my brother got tagged and if it hadn't been for you, he'd'a been shipped upstate? No. I can't do this 'less I'm sure. And I ain't sure."

Ms. Irene had also declined. "You know, Mali, this is not easy for me. I see a little similarity but not much. And there were several other delivery men at different times. I'm just not sure. Someone once said it was better to have a guilty person walking around free than to have one innocent person behind bars. And that's how I feel. I'm sorry, but I'm just not sure." I sighed and turned away from the drawing.

I like to think I'm considerate (most of the time) and somewhat well balanced (part of the time). And I try to keep my mouth shut if my opinion is likely to bruise someone's feelings.

I'm vocal about minor inequities, figuring if I scream loud enough I can prevent them from developing into major stuff.

I frown on displays of conspicuous consumption and tend to view modesty as a divine state. In short, I've got practically one foot (the good foot) in heaven and am pulling hard on the other. For this, I've received a few blessings in my life and I count Tad as one of them.

In bad moments I tend to squeeze my eyes shut and think of him. And depending on the occasion, my temperature either rises significantly enough to pull me out of the rut or it lowers gently to ease me into a semisomnolent dream state. I focus not only on his extraordinarily deep eyes and soft mustache and silver-edged hair but on his gentle nature, his goodness, and how wonderful he really is. I focus so hard sometimes that I have to pinch myself back to reality. He is my private oasis and his love is like a sweet water.

Most sisters would brag for days about the fine brother they've got draped on their arms. I never went that way, not even when Elizabeth first met him and then looked at me wide-eyed and said, "Girrrl, please! I see why you bumping into walls. You strolling half-dizzy!"

Yes, I am, I wanted to say but never did. I wanted only to remember that day at the precinct—I'd just reported for duty—when he had walked in, tall and broad-shouldered and dragging that fugitive, both of them covered with the dust and dirt of a sixteen-hour drive. I had looked beyond the layers of grime and chaos and I prayed, "Lord, don't let this fine brother be married. Don't let him be married. I'll die if he is."

Then I found that he was, and I didn't die but tried hard

to forget about him and to focus on the business of another cop, Terry Keenan, who was blocking me at every turn until I got tired of his nastiness and punched him out and lost my job.

I had never missed the job. I missed Tad. When he finally got his divorce and decided to part that beautiful mouth to say hello, really say hello, I had a hard time. I saw something close to perfection and it frightened me.

So I try not to measure other men by what I see in him. I remind myself that what the Temptations sing about is true: beauty is only skin-deep. I try hard not to focus on surface stuff but what lies beneath. Some days I'm good at it. Other days I flat out fail.

When Tad unfolded the sketches earlier, I had stepped back and failed.

"Damn. Just looking like this should be a crime," I said, regretting it as soon as the words left my mouth.

Now, as I stared at the pictures tacked to the wall, something stirred within my own memory. Or perhaps I had only dreamed it. Dreamed of seeing this face—not the face, but a fleeting impression, as one would a passing stranger exiting a subway or bus, never to be seen again. But when? Had I seen him at all or was the drawing so dramatic and I was staring so long that the image had imprinted itself in my consciousness?

I lay across the bed, trying to concentrate, to stretch memory. Perhaps the car accident had caused me to forget certain things. I had seen something, not quite like this sketch, but close.

❖

An hour later I sat up and eased my legs over the edge of the bed. The sun had vanished and the room was shrouded in gray. My leg ached but not enough to keep me from slipping into my sneakers and leaving the house again.

Outside, the sky had taken on the color of mottled silver and most people had retreated indoors. Lightning cut through the clouds and a faint rumble followed. I was practically alone as I strolled toward Malcolm X Boulevard.

At 130th Street the lights of the supermarket looked un-naturally bright, like a ship looming suddenly through a treacherous fog. I didn't know what I expected to find when I stepped inside, but something hidden in memory had drawn me here.

The aisles were nearly empty of shoppers and I wandered over to the frozen food section and gazed at the dozen vari-eties of ice cream: low-fat, no-fat, no-sugar, all-natural, all promising "rich" satisfying taste. My reflection, superim-posed on the small cartons, stared back, frowning. I turned away without buying any and walked toward the empty checkout counter, toward the empty place where image and memory suddenly came together.

He had been standing near the door that time, wide-eyed, scowling, and had turned away when I looked at him.

chapter

thirty

The humidity was so high by the time he reached 139th Street, his T-shirt clung to him and his face shone in the dampness. It was not quite rain, but heavy enough to persuade most people to retreat indoors to cooler, climate-controlled territory.

Ache lingered awhile on Eighth Avenue near the Sugar Shack and watched the door of the restaurant open and close and open again, allowing a faint strand of music to drift toward him in unconnected notes.

One couple, before they entered, leaned near the door to scrutinize the menu taped to the window and he caught their chatter—the man wanting a full dinner plus dessert, the girl reminding him of the need to watch his weight and select a sensible salad.

He eyed them and remembered that he had not eaten all day and the anger that brought him here rose in his chest again, nearly cutting his breath off.

He moved away quickly and turned onto 139th Street, walking east against the traffic pattern. The block was deserted, just as he imagined it would be.

Windows were closed against the humidity, and air conditioners hummed efficiently. The houses, trees, and streetlights appeared distorted in the haze. He walked slowly, not only to gain traction on the slick, leafy pavement but to check the windows of the parked cars and to spot anyone before he approached her house. The car windows were frosted with fine mist, so he gave that up and moved on warily.

Two nights ago, he had again gotten his foot on the bottom step when a car alarm had gone off and the dog started to bark. He had pivoted quickly and continued down the block without missing a beat. The alarm died when he had gotten several yards away, then suddenly he heard the pad of the paws and the dog growl directly behind him.

He froze. He had been too surprised to turn around and too paralyzed to run. He couldn't reach for the razor, and if he did, what good would it have done? If it was the girl and he got her, the dog would have gotten him. If he got the dog, the girl would have woken up the whole block.

But they had moved past him, the girl and the dog, walking so near he was able to see the glint of her small dark earrings, the pattern and whorl of her haircut. Her perfume, light and smelling faintly of flowers he could not name, drifted in her wake. He watched her walk. Had she been alone, he could have reached out and opened her throat in one gesture.

But that Great Dane. The animal was beyond big. It stood as high as her waist and its head was larger than most horses he'd seen. Its spotted black and white coat had gleamed under the streetlight as it trotted at her side. And she'd held the leash loosely in her hands like a trainer guiding a thorough-bred.

He had hung back, increasing the distance between them until they reached the corner.

Ain't this some shit. Just like last time. Damn dog make Godzilla chill. And she ain't movin' too swift. Like maybe her foot or leg or somethin' got spiked. Probably headin' for the park, but she ain't gonna do no whole lot a runnin', I can see that. Man, if that damn dog wasn't—

He had watched them move slowly across Frederick Douglass Boulevard and walk toward St. Nicholas Avenue, toward the park. The traffic light changed twice but he remained on the corner, watching until they disappeared.

She was definitely limping and he hoped she hadn't hurt

herself too badly because that's what he was supposed to do. No one was going to cheat him out of that.

Things different tonight. This damn soggy air. Need to go on and rain and get it over with. But rain or shine, the old man got a lotta gigs someplace and the limo probably picked him up by now.

He made his way to the middle of the block, treading on the slick pavement as if he expected to trip a land mine. One car moved down the street, its headlights throwing narrow spears through the haze, but it did not slow down. Somewhere in back of him, a few yards away, he heard a door slam, but when he turned, he saw that he was alone.

In the shadow of a full-leafed tree, he paused and again scanned the parked cars.

The house was directly across the street, and although he could not make out the detailed carving on the door in the faint reflection of the streetlamp, he knew it was the house. The windows downstairs were dark but lights shone through the blinds on the second floor. He waited, listening as footsteps approached, padding on the thin carpet of fallen leaves. An old man with glasses fogged by the mist walked past, turned onto Adam Clayton Powell Boulevard, and disappeared.

Ache was alone again and the hum of the air conditioners

came back, filling him with a sudden, alien feeling of apprehension. His shirt, boldly inscribed with "Don't Ask Me for
Shit," now clung to him in the moist air and made his skin
itch. Then he started to tremble as apprehension warred with
anticipation.

*I should ring the bell. Just step on over and ring it. If the kid
answer, say I made a mistake. Got the wrong house. And come
back some other time. No. Can't do that. Maybe he ain't home.
Maybe if he is, I take care of him too. No. The dog. The damn dog.
I been standin' here. Nobody walk him yet. Maybe . . .*

He drew his breath in as the lights came on downstairs
and the door opened. The boy stepped out with the dog at his
side. He watched the woman hand the boy a yellow jacket
and stand on the stoop. Her voice drifted toward him.

"Twenty minutes is enough. If it starts to rain, come right
back. I don't want you catching cold."

The background light illuminated her slim, long legs. She
wore denim shorts and a yellow cut-off T-shirt and she was
barefoot. Even without shoes, she was still taller than most
women, but that didn't matter. He watched as she closed the
door. He waited another minute for the boy and the dog to
disappear in the fog and then he glided across the street.

Ain't gonna miss this time. Can't miss.

Apprehension. Anticipation. It didn't matter. His heart
began the familiar racing and the dizziness came over him.
His stomach felt as if a snake had coiled inside. His chest was
pumping so hard he could feel it through the thin cotton

shirt. He smelled his sweat, stronger and more sour with each step he took. Finally he felt the tension, rare and exquisite, come up between his legs as he took the razor from his pocket, palmed it open in his gloved hand, and pressed the bell.

chapter

thirty-one

. . . Don't tell me that boy's back so soon. It took all evening to pry him away from that television just so he could walk the dog, now he's laying on the bell. Maybe it's started to rain. Where's his key? Why doesn't he use it?

"Hold on a minute!"

. . . I knew I should've walked him myself. I'd have taken him out earlier. Mama always said if you want something done right, do it yourself. Dammit, now there's the phone . . .

When I picked up the receiver, Tad's voice came on. He sounded low and thoughtful and I knew he was onto something. "Hey, baby. I'm at the supermarket, checking delivery slips. Did Claudine ever—"

"Tad? Hold it a minute. Alvin's at the door. He doesn't have his key."

I walked slowly toward the door, feeling the pain grip my leg with each step. Every time it rained or the humidity crept beyond a tolerable level, my leg acted as a barometer and I found myself thinking of James. His smiling face loomed large, crowding my thoughts, and in my anger I yanked the door open.

It happened so fast. The hand came down so fast I thought it was a bird, a bat, darting toward me. I fell back against the door, astonished. It slid past my face and I jerked my head and it slid past my ear.

Suddenly my shoulder felt as if someone had slammed it with a rock and red splashed down my arm. I looked beyond the bird into the face and the scream came from somewhere.

"Damn! It's you!"

The supermarket. The poster.

I stared at the face with the mouth drawn back and eyes bulging with a hatred churned up from some unimaginable place. Only a glimpse. I saw the razor and had no time to think, only to fight for my life.

His arm locked around my neck and I felt his weight against me as we wrestled through the foyer and into the living room. I dropped to my knees pulling him with me but he pulled me up again and we fell against the sofa, pushing it, heavy as it was, against the table, causing the lamp to fall over. The shade cast a slant of shadow against the wall and I battled to hold onto the hand that held the razor. The hand felt dry. He was wearing some kind of plastic gloves and he raised his arm, preparing to slice down again. We were face-to-face and his breath spewed out, thick and sour. I felt his spittle spray against my skin.

"Bitch! Make me lose my job! Come in there like you don't fuckin' know me! Like all them others! Fuckin' bitch!"

I didn't waste time or breath trying to figure out what the hell he was talking about. One hand, strong as a wrestler's, gripped my throat so tightly my vision blurred. I gasped for air and raised my knee and got him hard in the groin. He dropped the razor and I managed to kick it under the sofa. He fell back, doubled over. But only for a second, not in slow motion or freeze-frame, like in the movies. He rebounded so fast that when I stumbled behind the sofa, he was right be-hind me, his face bloated with rage. He had forgotten the razor and was coming at me with his hands.

"You ain't the first and ain't gonna be the last, you white-eyed—thought you could get away . . . !"

I leaped back and scrambled around the sofa, like a child in a manic game of musical chairs. "What the hell are you talking about?"

"I know you! Know your old man, your dog, your son. I know all about you. Came in for that ice cream. You know me! Yes you do!"

He was talking fast and the words spilled in a torrent of anger. "Fuckin' bitch. Just like that white-haired one. You know me and look right through me. Come in for that ice cream and look at me like I ain't nuthin'. None a you get away with that . . . None a you. I got everyone. Every time."

"Listen," I said, still moving, knowing he was beyond reasoning with. I needed to keep him talking, talking, talking. My arm was bleeding and my leg was about to cave in under me. Keep him talking. Keep him talking.

"What did the white-haired one ever do to you?"

I was yelling and he stopped short, apparently surprised that I didn't know.

"Plenty. That bitch did plenty!"

"What? What?"

I shouted again, trying to hammer through his confusion. He looked around, scanning the floor. "She—she—she was like them others. Mercy Anne and Natalie and all them others."

"Like the girl on Edgecombe? The girl on Seventh?"

"How you know that? See! I knew it. All along you was eyein' me. Those damn eyes. Make me lose my job."

He spun around, still searching for the razor. "Made me lose my job!"

Memory overwhelmed me and I knew I wasn't about to let this madman get me or get away. That was not going to happen. He didn't have the razor and I forgot about the pain in my leg. My arm was bleeding but I ignored that. I intended to fight to the finish.

Suddenly the phone beeped loudly and the operator came on. A recording that sounded almost absurd in this arena of overturned lamps and chairs and furniture dotted with blood: "If you wish to make a call, please hang up and—"

The line had been open. Tad had probably heard and was on his way. Maybe halfway here, turning the corner, running, flying, driving, he had to be almost at the door. If I could just keep him talking.

But he yanked the cord from the wall as I glanced around for something to defend myself with. Before I could reach for anything, anything at all, he cleared the sofa in a lightning move and shoved me against the mantel. His hands were at my throat, trying to loop the cord around my neck.

I clawed at his face but my arm by now was useless. My breath left me and I felt as if I were being submerged. I was drowning. My other hand scrabbled against the mantel trying to hold on. My head was exploding. I was underwater at a great depth and my lungs had blown up. I raised my arm and grabbed a piece of flotsam to try to keep afloat. I held on tight but the bulging, unblinking eye in the face loomed larger. I struck once, a swift powerful blow, before the waves closed over me.

chapter

thirty-two

I don't know who arrived first.

Tad, ready to shoot to kill, or Alvin, who aimed to maim. Maybe they burst in together. I don't know. I do know that Ruffin nearly finished the man off before Tad got Alvin to pull him off.

I ended up back in Harlem Hospital, where the doctor shook his head at the sight of my swollen neck, puffed eyes, and battered limbs and said he was going to start charging me rent.

I woke up in what appeared to be the same bed I'd occupied during my earlier vist. This time I had not gone into a coma although the blood loss had been significant. I had only, the doctor said, been choked nearly unconscious.

I gazed around the room as he stepped outside and said, "You folks can come in now, but only for fifteen minutes." And everyone seemed to crowd in at once. Dad, Alvin, Tad, Elizabeth, and Bertha. No one said anything. Elizabeth bit her lip, blinked, then burst into tears. Alvin followed. Bertha gazed at me and whispered something too soft for me to hear. Dad slipped into the chair by the bed and simply stared. For a minute, I thought he would start crying also.

Only Tad kept his composure, but the longer he stared, the more unsure I felt.

"Did I get him?" My voice sounded feathery, as if it wouldn't carry beyond the edge of the bed. My throat hurt when I spoke.

"Did I get him?" I whispered again.

Tad looked from me to Dad, then back to me again. "Mali. You got him. You got him."

"You did a job," Alvin said, recovering quickly so as not to get left out of the telling. I looked from one to the other. Dad had gotten up to console Elizabeth, and Alvin quickly slid into his seat and rested his elbows on the bed.

"Girl, you put his lights out," Bertha said, beaming through her tears.

"One light," Tad corrected, taking my hand. "When

we came in, the guy was on his knees howling, trying to pull Felicia's statue out of his face. His eye was enucleated.''

"What?" Alvin looked at him.

"Punctured. Completely punched out. Or in. Whichever."

"He's not dead?" I asked.

"No, but where he's going, he won't be needing twenty-twenty vision."

Tad passed his fingers lightly over my face and neck. "You're pretty well bruised up."

So that's what had everybody so upset when they walked in. They probably never saw a dark brown person that had turned blue. I closed my eyes to keep from laughing but opened them when Tad spoke. "Your legs gonna take a bit longer to heal. Last night's gymnastics sent you back to square one."

I nodded, not sure I understood. I closed my eyes and heard the doctor say, "Time's up. You can visit her again tomorrow," and I was grateful. All I wanted to do now was sleep.

This time it only took three days before I went home. I was supposed to remain off my feet for several weeks and Tad was only too happy to assume the difficult task of massage therapist. He was so dedicated he covered more territory than he needed and concentrated specifically on my hips and legs.

"My arm could use some attention also," I murmured at one point.

"Oh. Yeah. You're right. Just let me—"

That was the good part, those early-evening-into-late-night sessions.

The bad part was listening to the story of Charles Milton unfold. The fibers on his pants linked him to the Bronx murders but this forensic evidence was simply an overleaf:

Manacled to a bed in Bellevue's prison ward, he'd boasted of all the killings, swore he'd do it again as soon as he got out; that he wasn't finished because no one was going to ignore him and live.

He spoke of a Mercy Anne Tompkins and also of a girl named Natalie, left on a roof near 154th Street and Eighth Avenue. He wanted to speak to Geraldo, but since he, Ache, still had work to do, Geraldo would have to wait.

And every evening, the picture enlarged. Mercy Anne had been a classmate. Even though she had married and divorced, it had been easy for Tad to track her down. She had not moved too far from the neighborhood.

"I spoke to her," Tad said, "and she remembered Charles in junior high school. Said he was off the wall way back then. Said he always showed up late for school, when he showed up at all. And when he did, looked like something somebody had thrown away.

"Mercy Anne remembered Natalie also. Last name was Wilson. Natalie's mother had moved away after she disappeared, never knowing what happened to her daughter. Mercy Anne broke down when I told her what Ache had done, that he had killed Natalie.

"I went to the building where he said he had left her. The place had been renovated, done over about fifteen years ago, but the work had been done by homesteaders, sweat equity people, some of whom still lived there."

Tad coughed, as if his throat had gone dry. A minute later he continued.

"One old man, a Mr. Caeser, was sitting on the stoop and remembered when his crew cleared the garbage on the roof. 'We didn't know what or who it was,' he told me. 'Been there so long, nuthin' but bones. A raggedy dress and bones. I followed the case, kept after the cops, but you know how that is, just one more black child murdered and nobody give a damn.

" 'So me and the boys, we ain't had but so much—never did—that's why we was workin' for nuthin' to renovate the place. Sweat equity give us our own roof over our heads, our own homes. Anyway, we chipped in, passed the hat, and scuffled till we scraped together enough cash to keep that little kid from bein' put out there on Hart's Island. You know how they have that Rikers Island prison detail? They the ones bury them nameless people in that potter's field. Well, it wasn't gonna happen to this kid. Got thrown away in life but we wasn't gonna let that happen in death.

" 'Never did know her name or nuthin' but I know she restin' like she should. That's all I can say. That's all I can say.' "

Tad was sitting on the floor near the sofa, his hand resting on my stomach. He stopped talking and in the silence I heard Mr. Caeser's voice, heavy with age and emotion. Then that also faded into silence. I heard Tad cough again. He had turned the table lamp off and only the streetlight splintered dimly through the blinds.

I touched the side of his face and he eased my hand away. In the dark I heard—felt—him inhale.

"Natalie's in St. Raymond's Cemetery in the Bronx. I figure by the time you're mobile again, we could maybe take a run up there. See what's what."

"Okay," I said, waiting.

"By that time, her plaque'll be ready," he whispered.

I could not see his face in the dark but I imagined the small marble square, the piece of stone designed to give a nameless child back her past and embed her in someone's memory.

When Tad reached up to touch my face, he misunderstood my tears.

"You've been through a hell of a lot, baby. A hell of a lot. When you get on your feet, we're gonna make up for all the lost time we—"

"That's funny," I whispered, feeling the palm of his hand press against my midsection. "I thought we were doing that now."

"Oh no, baby. Not quite. Not quite." He rose and turned on the lamp, then went to his jacket that was draped over the chair.

"I wasn't supposed to mention this just yet, but I—"

We heard the key turn in the lock and Dad came in, saw the packet in Tad's hand, and said, "What? You told her already? I thought you were gonna wait."

Tad lifted his shoulders and I saw that rare smile. "Well, I figured this was as good a time as any."

I looked from one to the other. "What's going on?"

"Jazz cruise," Dad said. "I've got a gig on the *QE2*. Newport Jazz Festival. Lou Rawls, Aretha Franklin, Ruth Brown, Ron Carter, and whole lot of others will be there. This is the cruise of a lifetime."

"What?"

"That's right. We're all going. Tad has your tickets right there," he said, pointing to the packet.

Tad opened the packet and the tickets, traveler's checks, brochures, and tags fell out. "I told you we were gonna make up for lost time."

"This'll do it," I said, closing my eyes and thinking of Aretha Franklin. "This'll definitely work."